Mrs R.C. Waterston

Adelaide Phillipps, a Record

Second Edition

Mrs R.C. Waterston

Adelaide Phillipps, a Record
Second Edition

ISBN/EAN: 9783337002800

Printed in Europe, USA, Canada, Australia, Japan

Cover: Foto ©Andreas Hilbeck / pixelio.de

More available books at **www.hansebooks.com**

ADELAIDE PHILLIPPS

A RECORD

BY

MRS. R. C. WATERSTON

"THE echo of her voice enwrought
A human sweetness with her thought."

SECOND EDITION

BOSTON
CUPPLES, UPHAM AND COMPANY
Old Corner Bookstore
1883

Copyright, by
A. WILLIAMS AND COMPANY,
1883.

ELECTROTYPED BY BOSTON STEREOTYPE FOUNDRY.

PRESS OF WRIGHT AND POTTER PRINTING CO.

TO

Matilde and Arvilla Phillipps.

ADELAIDE PHILLIPPS.

CHAPTER I.

THE current of Adelaide Phillipps' professional life was bending towards a new channel when I first saw her. That moment is vividly before me now. She was standing beside Madame Arnoult's piano, having just finished her singing-lesson. Madame Arnoult presented her to me, saying: "Miss Phillipps is studying with me the songs in Cinderella; she is to appear in that part at her benefit." She was then about seventeen years of age, and seemed to me the brightest, healthiest, happiest young woman I had ever seen. I remember her showing me with girlish pleasure the play-bill, printed on

white satin, for her benefit, and won my
interest by her cheerful simplicity.

Madame Arnoult, a woman of fine
musical qualities and education, was then
the best instructress in vocal culture
in Boston.   Her husband, Dr. Arnoult, is
still remembered as a man of fine presence
and refined manners, whose instructions in
the French language were very much
sought and appreciated.   They were both
persons of good position in France, and
made many friends in America.   Madame
Arnoult knew the world, and especially
the musical world, and when she recognized the very remarkable gift Miss Phillipps possessed, in a grand contralto voice,
she advised her to study for the Italian
Opera.   Thus the lively and talented
young actress became a prima donna of
the lyric stage, a change not quite so
great as that of Cinderella, but something
like it.

Madame Arnoult took a truly mater-

nal interest in her young pupil, who became the companion and friend of the
charming Claire Arnoult, the daughter of
the house. At that time Madame Arnoult
resided near us, and we often attended her
musical evenings. She was surrounded
by a rare company of talented young
people, some of them her pupils: Adelaide and Claire, Theron Dale, Edward
Sumner, Harrison Millard, and others.
Sometimes these musical meetings were
held at our house, and thus began my
interest in Adelaide, which grew into
an unchanging affection. Miss Phillipps
had become well known and a great
favorite in Boston from the time when, a
mere child, she appeared on the stage
of the Museum; and when the change in
her career was proposed many were ready
to assist her in pursuing studies for a different branch of her profession. At that
time Jenny Lind was in Boston, — Jenny
Lind, who seems as remote to the present

generation as those mythical personages
Una or Chriemhild. Miss Phillipps was
introduced and sang to her. Jenny Lind
had a heart as well as a voice, and sent
her a check for a thousand dollars and a
letter in her own handwriting, recom-
mending Emanuel Garcia, who had been
her own teacher, as the best instructor,
adding most sisterly advice concerning
the career of an artiste on the lyric stage.
Many other friends came forward to show
their willingness to aid Miss Phillipps,
especially Mr. Jonas Chickering, the ever-
generous friend to all who appealed to his
sympathy, " especially to those who were
of the household " of music.

Miss Phillipps never wished to acknowledge that she was not an American by
birth, and even the fact that at Stratford-
on-Avon she first saw the light, was rarely
mentioned. Perhaps the very air of
Shakespeare's birthplace stimulated the
development of her infant dramatic powers.

Adelaide often said she did not know what circumstances led her parents to place her on the stage, but, at all events, she had no recollection of her first appearance, unless it was in a play where she was obliged to jump out of a window into somebody's arms. She was afraid to do it, until one of the actors standing in the wings held an orange towards her. She took the leap, and thus won her first prize.

Mr. Phillipps brought his family to America when Adelaide was seven years old. They went first to Canada, and afterwards came to Boston, where they remained. From her mother, who was Welsh by birth, Adelaide inherited many of her finest traits of character. The tender affection and unselfish devotion which marked Mrs. Phillipps' daily life in her family was an example her daughter faithfully followed.

Her father was a man of strong character, and watched over his children with a severe authority. Especially was this care extended to Adelaide. Placing her so early on the stage, he certainly performed his duty by guarding her from every danger through her early career. Very few young girls are so simple in manner and pure in mind as was this child, whose vocation brought her before the public. Through her long career she acknowledged that the stern protection of her father had always shielded her. But in her own nature there was a natural aversion to evil, which was a yet more powerful protection.

Mr. Phillipps' family were brought up in the habit of unquestioning obedience to their parents, which never seemed to cause any abatement of filial affection. The union between the members of the household was very strong, and continues unbroken, except where death has, from time to time, lessened their number, but never their affection.

It was in January, 1842, that she made her début at the Tremont Theatre in the comedy of "Old and Young," personating five characters, and introducing songs and dances. On the 25th of September, 1843, she first appeared on the boards of the Boston Museum, which then stood at the corner of Tremont and Bromfield streets, and had began to include dramatic performances among its attractions. The character which she assumed was "Little Pickle" in "The Spoiled Child." The song of "Since then I'm Doomed" is introduced into this play, and was given by her with much effect, being among her earliest lyric efforts. The exhibition of her budding histrionic powers were of course confined to juvenile parts, while her graceful dancing was a chief attraction at that early age. She was not satisfied with the position of a dancer, and thanks to the acuteness of the late Thomas Comer, then leader of the orchestra at the

Museum, she was soon promoted to show her capacity in such fairy spectacles as the children of Cypress, Cherry, and Fair Star, and later as Cinderella. For many of these the music was arranged by Mr. Comer. Her versatility of talent, readiness of wit, and obliging nature made her as much of a favorite behind the scenes as on the stage. "They were so kind to me," she would say, when speaking of those days, "they took such care of me, for I was but a child when I first appeared there, — so much of a child that I used to drive my hoop back and forth to the rehearsals. The work was play to me; I learned my parts easily, and was petted and praised, which was very pleasant." Besides the watchfulness of her father, she was much indebted at that time to her aunt, Miss Anne Reese, who was also connected with the Museum. She was devoted to Adelaide (her sister's child), and no memorial of the niece would be complete without some tribute to so excellent a friend and guardian. Her aunt continued to reside with the family until a late period, and Adelaide did not fail to repay in every way her obligations to this relative.

At the time of her early life in Boston, her parents resided in Tremont street, from whence one day, while driving her hoop to the Museum, she saw a beautiful doll looking out of a shop window. To possess this doll became the ardent desire of her heart, for which she determined to save every penny. Each day she looked at the doll, and each day seemed nearer to the purchase. But, alas! one morning the doll was not there, some one else had bought it. This was a terrible disappointment; the little girl ran to the Museum weeping bitterly, and reached the rehearsal in no feigned sorrow. Mr. W. H. Sedley Smith, then the stage manager, kindly inquired the cause of her tears, and the child's story touched his heart. He comforted her, not only with sympathy, but soon brought to her another doll as beautiful as the one she longed for. This kind gift was remembered with gratitude all her life. Beside her doll, the little brothers and sisters claimed her attention and were her pets. "I always remember mamma with a baby in long clothes on her lap, which she held so nicely; my youngest brother, George, was my special charge." She continued her care for him until she gave him a thorough education in the School of Technology. From Boston they removed to Neponset, to a house near the bay. Here they owned a boat which the brothers managed. On moonlight nights in summer the few residents near them used to listen to the beautiful voices that came from the little yacht floating over the water.

As Miss Phillipps grew up towards

womanhood she had many characters assigned to her. In those days there was
always a play and a farce at every theatre.
She often appeared in both. Mr. William
Warren was then, as now, the unrivalled
comedian, whose wit and pathos we all
know so well. In speaking of her experiences, Adelaide said, "I never lost the
command of my countenance but once on
the stage, and that was at the Museum, in
some farce where Mr. Warren was shut
up in a pantry closet, while I, apparently
unconscious of the fact, was playing the
piano accompaniment to a song. He
suddenly opened the door and looked out,
his face revealing the fact that he had
been solacing his imprisonment by help-
ing himself to some of the sweetmeats
on the shelves, assuming a look such
as only Mr. Warren could call up. It
was all over with me and my song; for-
tunately with the audience also, who were
too much convulsed with laughter to no-

tice my inability to proceed with my song until it was possible for the play to go on."

At the Museum Miss Phillipps continued a general favorite until, as has already been stated, a change came in her dramatic life. After many years had passed she came home one day and said with a good deal of feeling, "I have been to the Museum to-day, and there I saw the sword and shield with which I acted a Fairy Prince hung up as trophies. It is pleasant to be remembered." With much regret, although she did not swerve from the conviction that it was for the best, Miss Phillipps took leave of the Museum stage and the *corps dramatique* with which she had been so pleasantly associated. But the time had come.

In 1852, after a concert given as a tribute to her, at which she sang with other artists, she left home for England, accompanied by her father. They arrived safely in London, and took lodgings in Golden Square, a spot remarkable in the history of London as the residence of renowned people. Bolingbroke, the "St. John" of "Pope's Essay on Man," lived in Golden Square; also Mrs. Cibber, the singer of George II.'s time. Here also Miss Thackeray has made us all acquainted with the home of Angelica Kauffman in her delightful story of "Miss Angel." And now there came to Golden Square this young girl from America, to begin professional studies for a career on the lyric stage.

Miss Phillipps remained in London nearly two years, pursuing her studies with Garcia, and making good progress in the Italian language. It was a happy period of her life. Her master, Emanuel Garcia, took much interest in his pupil. He was one of those rare instructors who rouse all their pupils' energies. A brother of the immortal Malibran, he seems to have shared the magnetic charm of his sister, and, although a severe master, held a firm hold on all who came near his life.

After spending some time in London, Mr. Phillipps left Adelaide there and returned to America for a short visit. When he joined his daughter again in England, he brought with him the adopted child of the family, whose name, Arvilla, will often appear in this narrative. She was the daughter of a friend of Mrs. Phillipps, to whom she was entrusted. It should be stated here that, growing up into womanhood, it was a foregone conclusion that she should become the wife of Adrian Phillipps. At the time of her joining Adelaide she was a mere child, but so cheerful and happy that her companionship was a comfort to her sister, who, as will be seen in a few extracts from a journal kept during their stay in Italy, had her share of the varied experiences of a young artist at the beginning of her career.

In following the professional life of Miss Phillipps the record inevitably takes the form of a chronicle, being principally drawn from reports of the daily press in the various countries she visited. She never consented to any means being used by her agents to gain favor in regard to these reports of performances, and this fact gives force to the universal praise received from the press. Her letters contain little information except on personal or family concerns. The romance of stage life which may exist in the imagination of those who attend theatres does not form a part generally of the thoughts of the performers. To describe the effect of the lyrical dramas after the evening closes cannot be added to other exertions, and a sentence, " very successful," or " we are doing a good business," often is all that is written home by the weary Leonora or the martyred Azucena, although the applause of crowded houses yet sounds in

her ear, and she is surrounded by beautiful flowers as witnesses of the admiration
she had received.

In the autumn of 1853 Miss Phillipps,
accompanied by Arvilla and her father,
went to Italy, as a residence in that
country was thought best for her improvement in the Italian language, and afforded
an opportunity for receiving the training
of Signor Profondo in operatic acting.
This last study was less necessary from
her previous knowledge of the stage.
The grace and ease of every movement
of her perfectly modelled form, and the
light, firm tread of her small feet, must
be remembered by all who recall her appearance on the stage. A distinguished
clergyman of Boston (Dr. Bartol) says
in an essay recently published: "How
largely unconscious is all our best knowledge and lore of life. I said of a distinguished actress, Adelaide Phillipps, she
knew how to pose on the stage; and my

friend answered, 'She did it from instinctive grace, not knowing anything about it.' Was she less knowing because for the moment she was inattentive or unaware?"

Her grace was certainly instinctive, but she was seldom inattentive on the stage. One of the members of the Ideal Opera Company (Mr. Barnabee) illustrates this fact when he writes: "Among a large number of distinguished characteristics of her dramatic excellence was her absolute identification with the character she assumed, and her attention to the smallest details, to attain which she availed herself of any suggestions. I remember standing in the wings and observing the military correctness and precision with which she performed the operation of sheathing her sword in the *rôle* she was performing, and learned on inquiry that she had taken lessons from an army officer. Her presence of mind and ready

wit often extricated herself and her asso-
ciates from unpleasant predicaments. On
one occasion the last lines of her song es-
caped her memory (in Pinafore) and quick
as a flash, without lapse of time or rhythm
she supplied the words which set the audience in a roar, — 'The rest — I have —
forgotten.' It would, be superfluous for
me to comment upon her musical acquire-
ments or to write of her private worth."

Of the residence in Italy there is a
record in the diary alluded to, written by
Adelaide from time to time. The little
cahier lies before me in its blue paper
cover, the handwriting is that of a young
girl, and the record is touching from its
simplicity and truth: —

"FLORENCE, October, 1853.

"Commenced my diary for mamma.
Mr. Guerini said he had two new American
scholars, Mr. and Mrs. A——. We called
to see them and found them very agree-
able; they went with us to some place,

I forget its name. The next day they called and wanted me to go with them to see Michael Angelo's house, and also to see the making of mosaics, but I could not go on account of my Italian lesson. It rained this afternoon, and the thunder and lightning was dreadful.

"Mr. Biandi came and asked me if I wanted an engagement; he had spoken of me to one of the agents who wanted a contralto. The agent came accordingly. I sang to him ' *Pensa alla Patria.*' He seemed very much pleased with my voice. The place is Brescia, in Lombardy. They offer four hundred dollars a month for four months. The first part to appear in *Arsace.* Papa will give an answer in a few days. Mr. Biandi brought me the opera of *Semiramide* and gave me some good ideas. I commenced studying *Arsace.* 14th. Mr. A—— called and went with Arvilla and myself to the Pitti Palace. We were delighted. The pictures are superb.

Met Signor M——, who said it was an excellent chance for me to go to Brescia. An American artist (Mr. Jackson) asked, through Mr. Guerini, my Italian master, if I would sit for my bust to him, I said yes, and to-day he called, and I made an arrangement to go to his studio next Tuesday. Tuesday Mr. Biandi brought the engagement for me to sign, and told me I was to appear in *Il Vastale* instead of *Arsace.* He brought the opera and we read it over. Went to Mr. Jackson's studio in the afternoon. Evening, studied my part.

"SATURDAY, 5th of November, 1853.

Got up at four, left Florence at six o'clock, arrived at Pestoria, had breakfast, and arrived safe at Brescia; delighted with the place; made my début at Theatre Grande; had great success; opera *Semiramide.*"

The little diary breaks off, and for the story which follows, I am indebted to Arvilla's recollections, who was the constant companion of her sister. It was the custom of the place for the directors and musical critics to assemble at the theatre on the evening previous to the first representation, and expected a full-dress rehearsal. Signorina Fillippi did not wish to appear in the armor of *Arsace*, and with girlish obstinacy, persisted in coming on the stage in her black skirt and white overdress. The judges were displeased, and showed it. This put her on the defensive, and she sang through the part *demi-voice* to the despair of the manager. She certainly was not right to go against his interests and the custom of the place. The next evening the house was crowded. *Semiramide* was given and *Arsace* entered in full armor, but was received in silence. Not a hand was raised. She sang through the recitative and andante without applause, the directors and critics being determined to punish her for disobeying their edicts the evening before. But when she burst forth in the caballetta and threw into it all the passionate fire of her soul and wealth of her voice, she conquered her audience, and a storm of applause followed and continued during her whole engagement. A band of music awakened her early. the next morning, coming, as they professed, to congratulate her on her success, continuing to disturb her rest until they were *paid*, and then they went away!

The following is one of the many notices written in "La Fama," Brescia, December, 1853: —

"La Signorina Fillippi ('Arsace') por giovane e bella, ricca di forte e ad un tempo dolcissima voce, intuonata, flessibile, estesa, di vero contralto, educata al bel canto dal sommo institutore Emanuele Garcia destò un tempo piacene e marviglia. Lodossi pure il suo distinto ed elegante modo di porgene e l'anima di cui si mostra dotata e divenne in breve la delizà del publico, che le fece le piu clamoroso applausi."

Which may be translated: —

"Miss Phillipps is young and attractive, with a genuine contralto voice, rich and strong, at the same time of true intonation, sweet and flexible. The clear and distinct method of delivery, the soul with which she seems gifted, surprised and delighted us. She at once became the favorite of the public, who greeted her with clamorous applause. She is a pupil of the great master Emanuel Garcia."

"February, 1854.

"We remained at Brescia about four weeks, and then left for Crema, where we were to sing for the carnival. I had a letter from Signor Bottesini, the father of the great contra-basso player. He procured us apartments in the house of a friend, a Signor Freri. We were very comfortable there, and I had an opportunity of speaking Italian with the daughter, as she spoke pure Italian.

"It was very cold weather, the snow as deep as in America. The Impresario of the Milan Scala came down to hear me, and wished to engage me for three years; this I could not do, but was willing for one year. Signor Mangiameli also made an offer for the Carcano spring season. The last three weeks I was at Crema I enjoyed myself— walked with Signorina Freri every day; in the evening the theatre. Signor Buratti could not pay us at all; that rather threw us back. I was sorry to leave Crema."

Although there is no statement of the fact in the Journal, the same success attended her performances.

"Milan, March.

"As soon as we arrived in Milan we made an engagement for the Carcano. We were short of money, but thought we could get on with the pay I should have at the Carcano, but, unfortunately, we did not get it, and consequently we are not in a flourishing condition. I suppose it is all for the best. If I allowed myself the privilege I could sit down and have a good cry, but it would do no good. Mangiameli does not open the theatre, and I have no chance of singing. I expected Signor Mangiameli to-day at two o'clock, but of course he did not come. Well, he is thinking of me; that's one comfort! He told me last Saturday that he would open the Carcano on the 6th of June, and I should sing Romeo. ' *Chi sa ?* ' "

" March 25.

" Signor Profondo, who wrote wishing to make an engagement for April and May, does not yet appear. Three years ago yesterday papa and I left Boston. The weather is fine, and I sit with my window open. It is very discouraging to have no chance for singing and making some money. Well, I suppose it is all right, and this is a good lesson to me, so that if ever I am well off I may know what it is to suffer, and so help others."

This lesson, so trying to young or old, was learned and remembered, and in after

years, when success came, her heart and
her hand were ever open on every occasion where her sympathies were
enlisted.

To have made a successful début, and
then to be kept waiting for an opportunity
to reappear, is one of the trials of the profession, often caused by the jealousy of
rivals. After weary waiting, each week
promised an appearance, and nothing being
done, on Friday, 18th, the Journal goes
on: —

"Signor Mangiameli came. We went
with him to see the prima donna. She
asked me to sing at her benefit. I consented to sing the cavatina of Arsace,
'*Ecco mi al fine.*' La Signora M—— was
very kind to me. In the evening went
to the theatre; Signora M—— in a passion
about something broke a beautiful fan.

"The night had come in which I was
to sing to a Milanese audience. A very
good house; at the commencement of

the evening I sat in a box. At last I was
on the stage. They all looked at me.
Not a hand! I sang the recitativo without any applause; a faint *brava* once or
twice, and that they seemed afraid to do.
At the end, however, of the recitativo, I
had a good round of applause; then
several times in the adagio, at the end
of which I felt I had the audience with
me entirely.   The applause was so
great I almost forgot that I had any more
to sing.   During the cabaletta I could
scarcely utter a phrase but what they
would cry out and applaud me so that I
was in a perfect delirium, and sang as I
never sang before.   I was called out seven
times, and was obliged to repeat the cabaletta.   It was such a triumph as I did not
dream of having, much less hope for. I
felt very much like crying. Signora
M—— was very kind. She really seemed
pleased with my success. I could not go
to sleep until after four o'clock.

"Signor Mangiameli called before ten o'clock. I could not see him. We went to his office. There was a gentleman in the office talking about my singing. He said he had heard all the great singers sing the *Cavatina di Arsace*, but never as I sang it. 'I do not make compliments, but you have everything beautiful,—voice, execution, knowledge of the stage, soul, etc.' I thought that quite enough, and begged him to say no more. 'I do not flatter,' he said; 'all Milan is speaking of you.' On Tuesday I sang for the orchestra."

Although the entries in the Journal show much discouragement and waiting, yet that Miss Phillipps appeared in the Carcano Theatre is thus reported in "La Fama":—

"It is needless to say that the first honors were carried off by Miss Phillipps, who sang so beautifully the aria from Semiramide, better still the rondo from Cinderella, and exquisitely in the last scene from Romeo and Juliet. A shower of sonnets flooded the theatre after the rondo from Cinderella. We can truly say that Miss Phillipps has made a success in four short performances which would cost most artists a lifetime to acquire."

The little Journal records a wearisome waiting for the payments due and various engagements offered and not arranged. At last she writes, in March, 1856: "I made an engagement for Rovereto to-day. We are to be there a month. I cannot say I regret leaving Milan.

Monday, April, 1856. Several people came to see us off. We found the boat did not leave for Riva that day because it was *festa*, so we had to hire a carriage to take us to Peschiera, as the boat leaves there every day, festa or no festa. We met Signor and Signora Profondo at Peschiera. Signor Profondo says I ought to remain three years in Italy. At eleven

o'clock went up Lago di Garda, and arrived at Rovereto about seven in the
evening.

In Rovereto Miss Phillipps' success
was so great that it naturally excited the
jealousy of the soprano and tenor. On
the occasion of the tenor's benefit she had
no part assigned her, but was asked to
appear, extended on a couch, in one scene
where a lay-figure was needed. Of course
this proposal was declined. The tenor
and his friends spread the report that
Signorina Fillippi had refused to sing at
his benefit. Entirely unaware that any
adverse feeling had been excited against
her, Miss Phillipps came on the stage as
"Rosine" in the "Barber," a *rôle* in which
she had been received with much applause. Great was her astonishment on
being greeted with silence, and not only
silence, she heard that terrible sound
equally appalling to the traveller in South
American forests, or the prima donna on

the stage. She had self-command enough to go through with her song, but when she turned to leave the stage she burst into tears, such genuine tears as touched the emotional Italians. They repented the rebuke, convinced it was not deserved, giving her a round of applause which was renewed at every possible moment during the performance. It was the first and last time Miss Phillipps ever heard the voice of the serpent.

The following notice, translated * from a Rovereto paper, shows the place she held in the estimation of the audience: —

" Notwithstanding the bad weather the theatre was crowded with happy people. Great is the power which this young artist, with her superb voice and fine method of singing, has over the public. The applause which greeted her was immense. The flowers converted the theatre

---

* I am indebted to Mrs. Adrian Phillipps for these translations.

into a garden, and sonnets were showered upon her from over the house. It may be said in a few words that it was truly a festival."

One of these sonnets is selected from many others, and flows sweetly on the ear in that most musical language: —

All' Estimata Cantante
Adelaide Phillipps,
   Prima Donna Contralto
Al' Teatro Sociale di Rovereto,
   Nella sua serata di beneficio.

SONETTO.

Adelaide, tu canti! — E i mesti detti,
  Che l' angoscia d' amor strappa a' Elmireno.
  Eco destan gentile in ogni seno,
  Ricordo forse dei perduti affetti.
Adelaide, deh canta!   Benedetti.
  Sono i soavi tuoi concenti — Meno
  Non verra bella fama, e ognor, sereno
  Tu a te stessa cosi avienir prometti.
Canta Adelaide! — Che un' ebbreza pia
  La grazia dell' accento al cor apprende.
  E son gemelle, il sai, bellà e armonia.
  Canta! — Che il canto più sentiti rende
  Gioia, amore, dolor, malinconia
  In chi del canto la virtù comprende.

If the young prima donna could have fed upon sonnets, flowers, and applause her stay in Italy had been longer, and after patient waiting the success already achieved might have opened her way to a European career. The inducements to remain were many, — a delightful climate, the beautiful language, which she spoke and sang with ease and correctness, together with the demonstrative nature of the musical Italians, offered great attractions. But the Italian managers were unable to offer any salary worthy the name, and even that small payment was seldom made, and as we have read in the preceding pages, an opportunity to appear even after an engagement had been signed was hedged about with briers. Miss Phillipps possessed no means by which expenses could be met unless her engagements were remunerative. Under all these adverse circumstances it was decided best to return to America. At the

time we in America regretted this decision, considering it a great mistake.
The reports of her success reached us, but
not the records contained in the young
girl's Journal. We judged of what we
knew only in part. Another reason for
withdrawing his daughter from Italy ex-
isted in her father's opinion of the music
of Verdi just then becoming fashionable,
and which was of a nature too trying for
her voice, not having reached its full
power, and requiring careful treatment.
Whatever visions of her operatic fame
floated in the minds of her friends the
delight of going home was a reality that
balanced all other considerations in her
true and affectionate heart.

The public welcome on her return to
Boston was handsome. An extract from
one of the many tributes to her first appearance after her return, will show the
sincere welcome she received: —

"MONDAY EVENING, October 8, 1855.

"Miss Adelaide Phillipps was warmly welcomed. She has evidently profited much by diligent study under good masters, and will no doubt make a sensation in opera. The programme this evening gave the public five opportunities for judgment on Miss Phillipps' merits, and upon a most imperative encore she added her own pianoforte accompaniment, a sixth, which, in a new version of 'Home, Sweet Home,' expressed most feelingly her emotions on receiving the welcome home Boston extended to her."

A lively girlish letter written to her father while on a visit at Mr. W. H. Sedley Smith's house, who retained the interest she had awakened when a child at the Boston Museum, is full of her natural buoyancy. It is from West Groton, but there is no date of year or month, probably soon after her return from Italy: —

"DEAR PAPA, — Thinking you might like to receive a few lines from your unworthy, yet dearly-beloved daughter, and that you might be

alarmed and slightly agitated (enough to pre-
vent your hair from growing) at my non-appear-
ance at 'the dearest spot on earth,' I send
this letter to let you know that I am in excellent health and enjoying myself very much, and,
to be polite, I hope you are following my example. They wish me to remain here a few
days longer, and if you have no objection, and
are not, all of you, very unhappy at my absence,
I should be pleased to remain. Mr. Smith has
a very pretty place here; farm, I should say,
about fifty — what do you call them — of land
(acres?) and a pretty little cottage; four magnificent elms round the house, and a pretty lawn
before the *ditto* (is *that* the way to say it?).
Now I am sure after such a graphic description,
Rockwood (the name of the estate) must arise
before your sight in all its primeval beauty!
We rise about half-past six, and begin the day
by breaking our fast. We then walk through
the grounds an hour, read, make preserves,
walk on the lawn, dine at half-past twelve.
Then it begins to be rather warm; thereupon
we each retire to the place we like best and pass
the afternoon in reading or sleeping. Tea at
five o'clock, after which we wander on the banks

of the *Squmicook*, one of the most romantic
rivers I have ever seen ; sometimes we take a
boat and row upon its placid bosom. If you
passed through the adjacent woods you might
see two or three lovely girls refreshing themselves in its *liquid* waters ! What a fine thought !
At another time you might see a young girl
standing as one entranced gazing upon the beau-
ties that were around her, when suddenly you
would see her eyes — and graceful form — and
then her rosy mouth would open, and then such
a peal of celestial melody would break upon
your ear, that you would say it must be *Orfeo*
come to earth and goes seeking, in disguise, his
beloved *Euridice.*

"I have some idea of publishing my letters !
I feel it would do a great deal of good and be a
great acquisition to the literary world in form-
ing style and raising the tone of society, but I
do not wish it known at present, therefore you
will oblige me by not mentioning to the *literati*
that you have received this letter.   I would say
more, but it is time to send to the post-office.
The people are all talking round me, so that if
I had not been very much interested in my subject I should not have been able to express

myself so elegantly.   Mr. Smith, Mr. and Mrs.
Bigelow, and Miss Bellows, all desire to be remembered.   My love to Nanny and the children.

"I must now say adieu, and believe me your
affectionate   ADELAIDE."

CHAPTER II.

Miss Phillipps made an engagement in the spring of 1855 to appear in Italian opera in Philadelphia and New York. A fair prospect seemed opening for her début in America.

A few evenings before she was to leave town I had invited friends to meet her at our house. The day the party was to take place news came of the sudden death of her mother. My invitations were recalled, to the great disappointment of my guests and to my own sorrow. Knowing well the strength of the affection which united the mother and daughter, I felt that this bereavement must prove most unfortunate for Adelaide's professional future, coming, as it did, at so important a moment in the opening of her career.

She came to me in deep affliction. It was a painful task, and seemed a cruel one, to urge her to overcome the external emotions of her grief as far as possible in order to fulfil her professional engagements. She did so bravely, keeping down the fresh agony of a young soul's first great sorrow, to appear self-possessed before the rigorous public. Miss Phillipps made her first appearance in Italian opera in Philadelphia as Arsace, in Semiramide. One of the daily prints of that city thus reports the occasion: —

"Miss Adelaide Phillipps took the public by surprise last night by the classical purity and perfection of her execution in Arsace, which is one of the surest tests to which a contralto of the present day can be subjected. Miss Phillipps sustained herself triumphantly, and at once established herself as an artist of the first class."

An incident connected with that evening amused her in after years. Our friends, to whom we had written to insure their presence at her first appearance, as well as their sympathy for the trial under which she came forward, knew nothing of her previous history, and not much, perhaps, of the opera of Semiramide, and expected to see a trembling débutante in white muslin and blue ribbons. Great was their surprise when the young warrior, Arsace, came on the stage in full armor, helmet and sword, and acted the part with all the ease and fire of a practised artist. Her magnificent voice "brought down the house." Miss Phillipps fulfilled her engagement in Philadelphia, and returned to New York according to agreement, going through the representations at the Academy of Music. The following extract is from one of Edmund Quincy's letters to the *New York Tribune*, of which he was at that time a Boston correspondent, over the signature of " Byles ": —

" Miss Adelaide Phillipps' friends here have heard with great pleasure of the success which attended her *début* at the Academy. I am confident that it will increase the more you hear her. Her appearances in Philadelphia and New York were made under peculiarly trying circumstances. Less than a week before her appearance in Philadelphia her mother, to whom she was passionately attached, died suddenly, and it was in the midst of the most cruel affliction that she had to appear in obedience to the stern necessities of her profession. I think she cannot fail to fulfil the favorable impression of her first appearance after a short interval of calm and repose."

The severe strain upon her nerves during these performances brought on an illness which obliged her to shorten her engagement. During her stay in New York many friends were kind, but no one more devoted to her than Mrs. Sophia Morton Bullus, who from that time to the close of her own life ever extended towards Adelaide all the promptings of her generous and hospitable nature.

The unfavorable circumstances of her first appearance were such that her *début* in America can be fairly stated to have taken place on the 17th of March, 1856, under the management of Max Maretzek. The opera was "Il Trovatore,"—Miss Phillipps as Azucena. According to one critic, "this opera was new at the time, and 'Mlle. Fillippi,' as she was called, was really obliged to create the part. But it is not extravagant to say that her rendering of the character has always remained a standard."

This opinion is substantiated by innumerable tributes to her representation of Azucena in America and Europe. Only a few selections can be made from the mass of newspaper reports accumulated with regard to Miss Phillipps' representations of various *rôles*, all filled with discriminating praise.

The following extract, from a leading New York paper concerning the interpretation of the character of Azucena, was written during the season of 1856, and may serve as the impression ever made on the public by the artist in this *rôle:* —

"Miss Phillipps, when she appeared as Azucena, raised the Gipsy mother at once from a melo-dramatic personage to that of a tragic heroine. The paint and tinsel were eschewed alike with the artificial and exaggerated action so generally seen in the part. The vocal interpretation was rich, equable, and artistic, and the audience were again and again thrilled and inspired to irrepressible applause by the dramatic feeling she infused into the more declamatory passages, particularly in the *Condotta ell'era.* Bouquets were showered upon her, and round after round of applause."

It was in New York that Miss Phillipps sang for the first time " Leonora " in Donizetti's " La Favorita." " Her Leonora," writes an able critic, " became famous as the best that had been seen for many a day on the stage. Her performance was marked by noble delivery, able vocalism, truthful, impressive action, and unaffected pathos."

Those who witnessed her performance of the *rôle* of Leonora can never forget the effect of her graceful attitude when the curtain rose on the fourth scene of the third act. The resolution Leonora had taken of revealing her story to Fernando before their marriage gave noble elevation to her figure, as, after the recitative, she rose and advanced to the front of the stage, pouring forth, in her richest tones, the love, anguish, and hope contained in the cavatina, " *Oh, mio Fernando!* " In the last scene the lovers suddenly recognized each other in the court of the convent, both having determined to hide their sorrows in the cloister. Leonora finds that her letter discovering her story never reached Fernando. Enlightened now by her confession, all his feelings change and his love is restored. For one brief moment their voices mingle in the exalted strains of union and happiness which precede the death of Leonora.

There is a power of human passion and pathos in that scene which seems to have its counterpart in the meeting between Dimmisdale and Hester in the wood, as Hawthorne reflected it on the magic mirror of his wonderful romance.

A party of friends were one evening discussing the subject of different composers and their merits with Adelaide. There is always a battle waging between the adherents of different masters, be it in music or painting, and few of us are broad enough in our natures to acknowledge that though one side of the shield may be golden, and the other silver, they are both precious metals. One of the company said to Miss Phillipps, "you know some of the virtuosi call Donizetti's "Favorita" "trashy." Her eyes flashed, and sweeping to the piano, she struck a few chords, and then burst forth in a recitative and aria of that opera with a power, passion, and pathos which almost took the listeners off their feet. When the aria ended, she drew herself up with much dignity, and said, " Do you call that trashy? "

After a very successful first season in New York, Miss Phillipps was engaged for Havana by Maretzek. Havana then cultivated the opera among its tropical plants, and it was a city where artists were desirous of securing engagements. She immediately became the favorite contralto, and was received with unbounded applause. For three or four successive years the public demanded her re-engagement. A notice in an Havana paper, under date November 15, 1857, says: " Maretzek has taken the public favor by storm with his troupe. We have surrendered at discretion. Miss Adelaide Phillipps comes back to her place in our affectionate and respectful interest. She is the contralto favorite of Havana, and has found her way to our hearts." In speaking of Havana, in after years, Adelaide said:

"My greatest artistic success, my true appreciation, was in Havana." There was a touch of pathos in her voice as she recalled the friends she had there made and the experiences of her life during those seasons. She enjoyed the beautiful tropical regions, made various excursions into the neighborhood, and especially described a remarkable cave from which she brought us a beautiful specimen of stalactite. In Havana, however, she contracted the yellow fever, that serpent hid away among tropical flowers. She survived, but never entirely recovered from the effects of that terrible disease upon her fine constitution.

"The lyric stage," writes a musical critic, "was not the only one on which Miss Phillipps was eminent. In oratorio she was equally great, and in some respects unrivalled." She made her first appearnce before the Boston Handel and Haydn Society, December 30, 1860, in, the Oratorio of the Messiah. Her rendering of the impressive Aria, "He was despised," came not only with artistic power but from a devotional nature, and into the music she threw her soul, consecrating her artistic powers to the Source from whence all great gifts are bestowed. Equally beautiful was the expression which she gave to the words, " He shall lead his flock," as if in vision she saw the tender Shepherd carrying the lambs in his bosom, and was telling us the heavenly story in divine melody. Her next performance with the Handel and Haydn was in the " Stabat Mater," March, 1861.

Under the management of Signor Merilli, Miss Phillipps made a professional tour in Europe in 1861. She was accompanied by her brother Frederic, and arrived in Paris at the close of the summer. Paris was then, even more than at the present time, the great judgment-seat before which artists were to appear and receive sentence. Adelaide fully realized what an

ordeal awaited her in a first appearance
at the Italian Opera House, where Alboni,
the great contralto, reigned supreme.
There were friends in Paris who were
kind in their attention and cheer to the
débutante at this critical moment of her
life.   At the rehearsals Signor Mario, the
unrivalled tenor, who took the part of
Manrico in the opera "Il Trovatore,"
manifested much interest for her success.
He told the people behind the scenes at
the rehearsals that Miss Phillipps belonged
to an American city of great musical
knowledge and taste. "When Mme. Grisi
and I were there," said he, "so great was
the enthusiasm that the students from a
neighboring university volunteered to
come on the stage as 'Supes,' in order to
give expression to their pleasure in our
performance." "When the evening came
for the opera, I felt," she said, "for the
first time in my life 'stage fright' before
the curtain rose.   As I lay on the bank in

the opening of the second act, Signor Mario (Manrico) encouraged and roused me and dispelled to a degree the power of the demon."

The following letter is from the correspondent of the *Boston Advertiser*, under the date of Paris, October 25, 1861: —

" The musical portion of your readers will be glad to learn that Miss Adelaide Phillipps, as Signorina Fillippi, has passed through the severe trial of a first appearance before a Parisian public with entire success. The critical audience of the Salle Ventadour sat in judgment upon her 'Azucena' last night, and gave it their unqualified approval. Accustomed as they have been to Alboni, and no one else in this part, it was not to be expected that they were to experience any new sensation in the rendering of the music. To achieve success it was necessary to make *it a dramatic* triumph. Alboni, with her wealth of voice, is so fat that she can only stand still while the music gushes from her throat like a fountain. Miss Phillipps, on the other hand, has a great deal of dramatic power, and displayed it to such purpose in her delineation of the fierce, revengeful, yet loving gipsy mother, that she would have made a hit with far less vocal excellence than she possesses, for the French like *acting* above all things, and Alboni is one of the few whom they would tolerate without it. Miss Phillipps had several difficulties to contend against ; — a feeling of awe at the proverbially severe and cultivated character of a Paris audience, and a sense of the important results their decision would have on her future career, were surely not unnatural even to one accustomed to the stage from her earliest years.

"There is something appalling in the way a débutante is treated here on a first night. There is no token of a greeting. The first movement begins and ends, and then the second, and still there is a chilling, unsympathetic silence. At length at the end of the cabaletta there is a moment of suspense. The applicant for favor has been heard and judgment pronounced. For one instant she is doubtful if it is to be a blank or a prize, the suspense lasted an instant only, for there followed a burst of applause that must have satisfied the most anxious friend or most ardent admirer.

"Some injudicious friend threw a wreath as large as a horse-collar on the stage before Miss Phillipps had sung a note. This awarding of laurels before they were earned puzzled the audience and embarrassed all on the stage. They did not know what to do with it, till at last Mario picked it up and threw it behind the scenes.

"Miss Phillipps was called out after the first act, and at the close of the opera; a mark of approbation not often bestowed. This success is an 'Open Sesame' to her for every opera-house in Europe, and she may well congratulate herself on such an important step in her career. Mario never sang better in his life.

" Miss Phillipps makes her second appearance in the "Ballo in Maschera," again taking Alboni's part. She will also appear with Penco in "Semi-ramide" as Arsace, where she is quite at home in a part especially adapted to her, both vocally and dramatically."

Galignani says of Miss Phillipps' début, " she took the public by storm, and the result was complete success."

The Paris correspondent of the London *Morning Herald* thus analyzes her gifts : —

" A noble contralto voice, a style remarkable for its *brio* and pathos, perfect vocalization and powers as an actress, only to be compared with that of Malibran and Madame Viradot, are the recommendations of Mlle. Fillippi to the favor of the public. Her success was immense."

The Paris *Patrie* of 1861 extols Miss Adelaide Phillipps as the best contralto that has been heard in France for a long time. "*Voilà un vrai contralto;*" and to these qualities it adds: —

"She joins a rare energy and spirit as a *comédienne.* She is of the very best order, and must soon eclipse by her magnificent talent certain artists who now stand high in the public regard. Miss Phillipps won her first laurels in America. Her reputation will soon be European."

Miss Phillipps' season at Paris was so successful that the impresario of the *Italiens* engaged her for the whole season of the next year. From Paris she went to Spain, under the direction of Signor Merilli, with a troupe of which Madame La Grange was the soprano. She sang through the opera season in Madrid with distinguished artists, and held the various contralto *rôles* of the favorite operas, always sharing the applause which followed the representations, and sometimes awakening jealousy by a greater success than débutantes are generally allowed to obtain. She was in the midst of this gratifying career when news was received that the impresario of the Italian opera in Paris had played with false cards.

Gamblers it seems draw the line at false cards, and it was a breach of honor that could not be overlooked. The impresario of the opera in Paris is the servant of the government, and he was dismissed from office. His successor was not bound to fulfil previous engagements; he had other prima donnas on his list, and Miss Phillipps lost this valuable opportunity in her artistic career. She bore the great disappointment with the same good

temper and dignity that she manifested
through all the trials of her professional
life.

The climate of Madrid is very cold and
trying to vocalists, and Miss Phillipps
hardly dared to venture out, or to visit the
picture-galleries, or enjoy any of the pleasures of a traveller. The severe climate
of Madrid made her dread that of Russia,
and she declined offers of engagements in
St. Petersburg, where doubtless she would
have achieved fame and fortune. The
recent death of the charming Madame
Bosio, in that country, from illness contracted in a journey from Moscow to St.
Petersburg, had a great influence on Miss
Phillipps' decision to avoid Russia.

She was also offered an advantageous
engagement in Brazil, but did not accept
it.

CHAPTER III.

FROM Madrid she visited Barcelona
and various cities in Spain with the opera
company, returning to Paris in the spring
of 1862. She was at once re-engaged by
Merilli for an extended professional tour
through the north of France, Belgium,
visiting also Holland, Poland, and other
parts of Europe. She was the star of the
company. Everything seemed to favor
her, and she enjoyed the whole journey,
not only its professional success, but she
felt a vivid interest in the countries she
visited. Her quick eye caught all their
beauty, and she appreciated the history of
the great past which was associated with
many of the places through which she
passed. The old cities of France welcomed her; at Lille so great was her

success that the press of the city presented her with a laurel wreath at her
benefit.   Near one of these cities the
leading members of the troupe were
invited to visit a family residing in a
neighboring château or castle, of which
Adelaide gave, on her return home, a
graphic description. ´ The building was
very old and picturesque, with a tower
which had stood a siege. "I never understood," said she, "of any place what
people meant when they said it was like
being in a play, until I looked out of my
window on this old tower, with its moat
and surroundings.   The family, who must
have been of rank, were charming and
hospitable.   They seemed to live much
of their time in this château, but were
great patrons of the opera when any
troupe visited the place, and often invited
the leading artists to their house."   This
was a very pleasant incident in the tour.
When performing in one of the cities of

Poland she was much impressed by the fact that all the ladies present at the opera wore black dresses as mourning for their country! In Poland she visited a salt-mine, one of the noblemen in power having ordered it to be illuminated in her honor. She described it as a fairy scene, unlike anything out of the Arabian Nights. At Prague she had immense success, especially when she performed " Zerlina " in " Don Giovanni."

That opera was originally written by Mozart for production at Prague, and its performance there is always attended by unusual popular interest. On this occasion of the representation of Don Giovanni the demand for seats became so great that the town theatre was abandoned and a summer theatre beyond the city limits was utilized. The road to this place the evening of the representation was thronged early. When the opera was to be performed, Miss Phillipps and the rest of the troupe dreaded the ordeal, but her success as Zerlina was indisputable, and that night has since been memorable in the musical annals of Prague.

Her visit to Hungary, especially to Pesth, interested her extremely. If the pen could only convey Adelaide's brilliant and vivid descriptions of all she saw and experienced on this tour, aside from her success as a prima donna, these pages would be luminous indeed.

At the close of this engagement Miss Phillipps returned to America. At home we were in the midst of the war of the rebellion, and if not, like the ladies of Poland, in mourning for our country, we were sorrowing over many brave and beloved ones fallen in her defence. Adelaide had her part also in the anxieties of the time, as her brother Adrian was on the staff of Admiral Thatcher through three years of the war.

While in New York, during an opera

season, she was the guest of Mrs. Sanford. The following letter addressed to her sister, is dated —

I take a large sheet of paper, for the good reason I have not a small one at .hand. I am getting on well, the weather is pleasant, and *Martha* was a success. I have received congratulations from many for my great success in it. So I suppose it is all right. Last evening Adrian came ; was delighted to see him; looks well, though he is home on sick leave. Parepa sang in a concert last evening before the opera (*Lucrezia*), and we had the pleasure of commencing after half-past nine o'clock. I had to sing my *Brindisi* three times, although it was more than half-past eleven o'clock. Mrs. Sanford's maid goes with me behind the scenes, I have always two or three young ladies also, so you see I am well protected. I had a very pleasant ride on horseback this morning, at seven o'clock, in the riding-school with Mr. Stanfield. He wished me to try his horse in the ring first that I might have no fear. I like the horse very much. Adrian went with me. We took a long walk up Fifth avenue, and arrived at home in time for breakfast at nine o'clock. Adrian will leave for Boston to-morrow night. Adrian has told you all the news, nothing particular has happened since he left us. Friday morning Mrs. Sanford and I went to riding-school, and had a very pleasant ride. In the evening went to the opera, *Norma;* a fine house. Saturday had a most lovely ride in the Park on horseback of course, we left home at seven o'clock; the weather was delicious. Last night we all went to bed early. I hope Adrian will return to New York; tell him to be sure and write to me. Remember me to the Websters. I suppose you will all be having a good time on Tuesday, as it is Carrie Webster's birthday. Love to every one; shall be most happy to hear from any one who will take the trouble to write to me. Adieu.

Yours affectionately,

ADELAIDE.

In the spring of 1864 Miss Phillipps was re-engaged for Havana, under Signor Lorini's direction. She was most cordially received there, repeating the *rôles* in which she had been so great a favorite, and reviving friendships gained a few years before. It was in Havana that she obtained those charming Cuban songs which all who heard them will remember, dropping like the princess' jewels in the Arabian nights, sparkling and bright from her lips. These she often introduced in response to recalls after her grand arias, the liquid, lustrous tones having the rhythm of fairy bells.

It was in her earlier visits to Havana that Adelaide obtained her knowledge of the Spanish language, which she spoke with fluency. Mr. Charles F. Bradford, of Roxbury, himself an able Spanish scholar, in speaking of Miss Phillipps said: "To converse with her in Spanish was a rare pleasure; the ease and grace of her language, the beauty and vivacity of her conversation were fascinating. You know," he added, " how I admired her as a vocalist, and esteemed her as a woman; the perfection of her Spanish made the charm of her society complete."

Miss Phillipps took the contralto part in the oratorio of " Elijah " for the first time in 1864. It was during a visit at our house that she prepared for the oratorio, and studied the score carefully. " I must take it in at my eyes," she said, " before I go to the piano." The exquisite aria, " Oh rest in the Lord," ·impressed her very deeply, and must ever be associated with her voice by all who remember its tender tones and expression. She once said, "You do not know how much that aria has been to me; whenever I feel sad or depressed I go to the piano and sing it to myself; it always comforts me."

Another association with these sacred words must find mention here. At the services given at the Music Hall, in commemoration of Charles Sumner, June 9, 1874, Adelaide Phillipps sang "Oh rest in the Lord." Fit expression for a soul whose " heart's desire " that slavery should be ended had been granted; whose battles were fought, and who after victory had found " rest."

It was on a professional journey to California in 1865, while crossing the Isthmus, that Adelaide made the acquaintance of our friends, Mr. and Mrs. Charles W. Huntington, of Boston. Mrs. Huntington's fine musical taste had appreciated the artistic powers of Miss Phillipps, and the knowledge of her personal qualities caused a sincere friendship to be formed which continued through the following years. On their return to Boston the hospitable house of Mr. and Mrs. Huntington became one of Adelaide's homes.

The opera company with which she was connected had a successful season in San Francisco. There are many tributes to her performances in that city. Here is one which expresses the general admiration she won, for, unlike the bouquets showered upon the prima donna, these

warm-hearted expressions do not lose
their aroma by time: —

"The benefit of Miss Phillipps on Wednesday
evening was all that lady could expect, as the
Academy was densely crowded. 'The Barber'
was given and accepted with equal zest and
relish by both artists and audience. The last act
of Romeo and Juliet was sung very effectively by
Miss Phillipps and Signorina Sconcia as the conclusion of the entertainment of the evening.
Miss Phillipps as Romeo gave the audience a very
strong evidence of her tragic abilities. She was
honored by a bewildering profusion of flowers,
together with a white dove which fluttered down
to her, going through his part very gracefully.
Some very beautiful specimens of California gold
wrought into ornaments were also presented,
while the receipts of the house gave California
gold in another shape — to the amount of over
two thousand dollars."

Through the seasons including 1865 to
1868, she appeared in opera and concerts,
visiting California, the Western States,
Chicago, Philadelphia, New York, Boston,
and many other places, travelling thou-

sands of miles and giving almost as many performances. Chicago thus greets her in October 30, 1857: —

"Miss Phillipps as Rosina gave an artistic and finished representation of coquettish character. Light, vivacious, and thoroughly at home on the stage, her acting may be as warmly commended as on the preceding evening in a totally different portraiture. Her versatility is surely evinced in the perfection with which she equally represents the passionate gypsy, and the coquettish ward of a petulant guardian. Certainly Rosina has never been given us in her twofold character of what she is and what she appears to be to Dr. Bartoldo as Miss Phillipps embodied her. For pure, sympathetic, solid vocalization it has never been surpassed. In the music-lesson scene she introduced a Spanish song with a very quaint and charming orchestral accompaniment, which was warmly encored."

The family to which Adelaide belonged was a musical one, and her sister Matilde had developed a noble contralto voice. One morning Adelaide came in quite excited and said, "I have been hearing

Matilae sing. Upon my word I must look
to my laurels; she has a grand voice. I
never intended her to be a professional
singer, but she has the true artistic tem-
perament, and I must give her every ad-
vantage, and shall go to London and place
her with Garcia next summer." Adelaide
was at that moment studying the parts
she was to take in 'the great Triennial
Festival of the Boston Handel and Haydn
Society, May 5, 1868. Of the opening of
this Triennial Festival the following report is taken from the *Daily Advertiser*
of that date: —

"The present festival has been planned on a
larger scale than any kindred undertaking in
this country. . . . The soloists that will appear
from day to day include the best talent procur-
able, headed by Mme. Parepa Rosa and Adelaide Phillipps. There was a brilliant audience
at the opening of the festival. The performance of Mendelsshon's 'Hymn of Praise,' justified
the promise of the rehearsal. Parepa Rosa and
Miss Phillipps were in superb voice. The chorus

* By Mr. Howard D. Ticknor.

and orchestra were very effective and Carl Zerrahn as leader deserved great praise on the occasion. The oratorio of Samson was given in the
evening of the opening day, Mme. Rosa in the
soprano, Miss Phillipps in the contralto *rôles.*
If the soprano's music was rendered with fitness,
so also was Miss Phillipps' in the contralto music
of Micah. One of the first canons laid down to
us by an old master of the genuine classic school
long years ago was that, except where words were
merely added to music as a vehicle for carrying
on vocalization, the spirit of the words should
always be paramount, and the music so tempered
as best to illustrate the text for which it was
composed. Miss Phillipps sings as if this rule
were ever in her mind when she assumes an
oratorio *rôle,* or indeed any *rôle.* Her noble
voice, her high culture, and her clear, crisp, real
execution are never forgotten, but she always
sings as if she meant what she is singing, and
only used music as a help to full expression.
Her "Return, O God of Hosts," and "Ye sons of
Israel now lament," were perfect in feeling and
coloring, and in our mind the very gems of the
performance. Her recitatives were also admirably read."

"On Friday afternoon of the week Beet-
hoven's Ninth Symphony was given. There can

be no more crucial test of singers and orchestra, and if ever that test was nobly and gloriously borne it was so yesterday.   The three first movements were splendidly sustained, and when the great finale began to rise in cumulative strength and sublimity every individual chorister or instrumentalist seemed imbued with positive inspiration to meet and triumph over the tremendous exigency of the time.   The solo passages were worthy of the master and the hour in their sureness and strength, delivered as they were by Mme. Rosa, Miss Phillipps, Mr. Stimpson, and Mr. Rudolphsen."

The festival ended on Sunday evening with the oratorio of the "Messiah."   The writer already quoted closes his report of the week as follows: —

" Although the climax of this festival must be held to be that wonderful presentation of the Ninth Symphony, yet the Messiah of last night was worthy to rank with the best versions of that great work, and worthy to conclude a series of performances, which, in the entirety of their scope and rendering, have never — as we think we may in no boastful spirit assert — been approached on this continent.   With that splendid orchestra, that mighty sea of organ tone, that immense chorus, with its enthusiastic, urgent, yet generous and wise conductor, that quartette of principals, — with all these elements what could but result in unqualified success last night? With our minds reverting, as we write, to the emotions and incidents of the last few days, we cannot enter into details of this last performance to tell at length how Mme. Rosa uplifted and swayed all hearers, how Miss Phillipps' pleading voice gave new pathos to her touching arias, nor how the smooth sweetness of Mr. Simpson's tenor, nor how the strong, honest bass of Mr. Whitney supplemented and supported them ; and our one general, genial heartfelt tribute must go on record thus simply and shortly."

In addition to the oratorios Miss Phillipps sang at two concerts, in one that pathetic song from Handel's "Rinaldo," *Lascia ch'io pianga*, which was exquisitely rendered.

In the summer succeeding the Triennial she went to London, as has been stated, and placed her sister satisfactorily with

Garcia as instructor. She visited Paris, and made an engagement for the next winter, which she afterwards cancelled on account of the illness of her father.

In February, 1869, Matilde Phillipps was summoned home by the wish of her father to see her once more. She obeyed, and crossed the Atlantic alone in the midst of winter. Adelaide was at our house awaiting her. By some mistake no one was on the wharf to receive the solitary traveller, and unable to understand what this meant, she was kindly attended by a fellow-passenger to a hotel, from whence she drove to our house to hear some intelligence of her family. Adelaide received her. Matilde was quite worn out with fatigue and excitement, and, indeed, needed a comforting reception.

She had then been nearly a year under the instruction of Garcia, and, of course, we looked forward anxiously to hear her voice. The next day I told her how de-

sirous Adelaide was to hear her sing; but,
knowing artistic temperaments, she would
not urge her to do so. After much hesi-
tation, Matilde said: " Oh, I would rather
face a thousand strangers than sing to
Adelaide! How should I feel if, after all
she has done for me, I should disappoint
her?" At last she took courage, and
asked her sister to play the accompaniment
of *Di tanti palpiti.* I retired into the
next room in order to leave the sisters together, taking care to be near enough to
listen, and, as the beautiful voice and fine
rendering of the recitative and aria fell on
my ear, I felt that gratification had come
to us all. As the last notes of the accompaniment died away I re-entered the
room. Adelaide turned to her sister, and
said in her emphatic voice, "Matilde, I
am satisfied, more than satisfied." It was
a touching moment. I believe we all
wept. What else could three women do
at such a moment? To Matilde it was

deeply gratifying, and scarcely less so to
Adelaide.

Some one says that joy is so foreign to
our experiences that we can only express
it by our tears.

Matilde went to Marshfield, where her
father's pleasure in seeing her rewarded
the effort she had made. After a short
visit she returned to London, and continued her studies, and from thence went
to Italy, where she made her début, and
continued in Italy and Sardinia several
years with much success.

Whenever Adelaide's public engagements allowed her the pleasure of spending a few weeks socially among her many
friends she enjoyed their home and their
society life very much. Her buoyant spirit
and many accomplishments rendered her
always a welcome guest. The subjoined
letter, addressed to her sisters, was written during a winter visit to Mrs. Dr.
Doremus, in New York:—

"NEW YORK, 70 Union Place.

"MY DEAR GIRLS, — Why don't you write to me. I am really worried, for Adrian promised to write as soon as he had seen you all, but not a word have I received. Send me a few words immediately. You remember, Arvilla, the music I left in your charge at Marshfield. I want you to send the orchestra parts (and piano) of 'Orfeo' and the 'Barbiere,' also the 'Bacio.' Send immediately. I am going to sing at a concert here, Gosche engaged me; now remember. I suppose you wish to know what I have been doing since I wrote last, I think on Saturday; so here goes!

"That evening we went to see Booth; had a private box. After the performance the gentlemen who went with us came home to supper. I sang a few little things. Sunday we went to church, and I dined with Mrs. Sanford. Several people there, among others, Kate Field and her mother; pleasant evening, music. Monday, rained all day. I practised a little and wrote two or three letters, and in the evening we went to see Owens in Solon Shingle at the Broadway Theatre, met Guerrabella there. Tuesday went to see Mrs. Sanford, took a pleasant walk, and in the evening went to the artists reception; met everybody I had ever known. Wednesday,

Mrs. Doremus' reception, great many people.
Sang of course, was in very fine voice. Had
a handsome present of flowers, and a nice
dance. Made Mr. H—— dance the lancers
with me. Thursday, pleasant day. Evening,
went first to Mrs. Wilson's to hear Hoffman
play, then to a party at Mrs. Mackay's, had a
lovely dance. Friday, went out, made calls.
Evening, had a quiet time at home, that is to
say, only about a dozen people came to see us.
Saturday, went to the Philharmonic. Adrian
came and found me there. I need not tell you
what we did that day. Adrian must have given
a description. Sunday after Adrian left I dined
with Mrs. Stevens and Miss Reed. They have a
magnificent house. It was a regular dinner-
party, and very elegant, which they appeared to
give for me. We had music of course. Monday, went to see Mrs. Moulton. You have heard
me speak of her. She was Miss Greenough, and
married in Paris. While there met Mrs. Hills,
who invited me for the next evening at her
house. Mrs. Moulton was to be there. On
Tuesday I went and had a delightful time. Miss
Reed, Mrs. Moulton, and I sang, also the young
lady of the house. I suppose many of the
nicest people in New York were there. Dr.
Doremus and I took Mrs. Moulton home. Be-

fore going out Gosche called and I made the engagement to sing at the concert. Wednesday, went to see Mrs. Sanford. Evening, Mrs. Doremus' reception, music, dancing, etc. Max Strakosch came to see me, and wants me to go on a concert tour. Evening, went to a free school to hear Dr. Doremus give a lecture on chemistry. I sang an English song to the children. Friday, went with Mrs. Sanford and Guerrabella to Fifth Avenue skating-pond. Lovely, mild day. Very good skaters. Evening at home. The laughing song has made a perfect furore here. Why does not Mrs. Ring send my dress? I want it particularly for Tuesday, a dancing-party I am going to. There, now you know all about me.

Yours,   Adelaide."

The allusion in the preceding letter to her "singing to the children," illustrates one of Adelaide's characteristics. She was very fond of children and had a great charm for them, as they generally have the power of thought-reading, and recognize the real friend. A party of young girls, graduates of the Everett School, who met her one afternoon at our house, each doubtless remembers, through the years that have intervened, how gayly she entered into their pleasure, and sang for them bright and lively songs. In her last evening visit to us she described, with wonderful vividness, a little girl who was once a passenger with her in crossing the Atlantic, — a wilful, unmanagable creature, full of the very spirit of mischief and insubordination. Adelaide determined to subdue her, and through resolution, and the magnetism of her power, the child become gradually more and more under her influence, and at last sat quietly at her feet, and looking up in her face, said, " You have made me good, though I did not mean you should." All who as children were brought in contact with Adelaide in their homes (now perhaps with children of their own) will recall many anecdotes of her delightful companionship, and hold those memories among the sweetest of their childhood. Hers was a broad nature, stretching out its sympathies on every side, touching the electric chain by which we are bound to each other, sending the message of cheer and comradeship along the line whether in sunshine or in storm. The influence of her song upon untrained natures was shown one evening at a fashionable house in New York, where Miss Phillipps sang Kathleen Mavourneen to a large company. While the song proceeded the young waitress came into the room with a tray in her hand; the pathos of the voice and the song entirely overwhelmed her; and, forgetful of time and place, the girl sank down on a seat and burst into tears. It was a heartfelt homage to the singer.

The great "Peace Jubilee" took place in Boston in the summer of 1869, an immense building having been erected for the purpose. It was a time of great excitement. The war of the rebellion was victoriously finished, sanctified by the proclamation of freedom which ended slavery in the United States. Some public demonstration seemed fitting. The whole affair was arranged with much care, and was a success. A great chorus and orchestra was led by Carl Zerrahn, and the performances were worthy of the occasion. Mme. Parepa Rosa as soprano, and Adelaide Phillipps as contralto, were the leading artistes, but many others filled the *rôles* needed in so vast an undertaking. Miss Phillipps spent the week of the Jubilee with us; and as we drove every day to the private entrance of the building it was interesting to see the ripple of pleasure pass over the faces of the crowd as they recognized her. Few of them could enter the hall, but their expression of good-will was more gratifying than the loud applause of the multitude within. The immense size of the auditorium raised a doubt if any one

voice could fill it. One of Miss Phillipps'
friends, at her request, stationed himself
on the upper tier of seats. They agreed
upon a signal to testify if her voice clearly
reached him. The signal was made at
all the doubtful points very satisfactorily.
Mme. Parepa Rosa's voice rose finely,
and her whole appearance seemed in harmony with the occasion. The press
speaks most favorably of all the performers. "On the second day," says the *Transcript*, "Miss Phillipps was the soloist
in 'non più di fiori,' which, though not
suited to such an immense audience-
room, was faithfully rendered by Miss
Phillipps, and her charming delivery of
the air was recognized by every cultivated listener."

On June 18th the attractive programme
was given to the children of the public
schools. Mme. Rosa sang "Hear, oh
Israel," Miss Phillipps, the song from Lu-
cretia Borgia, "Il segreto per esser felice,"

and both prima-donnas joined in the
duet from Stabat Mater, "Qui est Homo."
As memory recalls those two distinguished
women as they stood together on that great
platform, and hear again the echo of their
grand voices, it is hard to believe that
they have passed away from the music of
this world forever.

Of the closing day of the great Jubilee,
June 19, 1869, the same writer gives
this tribute to Miss Phillipps: —

"We are glad to say that her superb artistic
reputation was reached in 'Lascia ch'io Pianga.'
She never sang more nobly and truly. Her
voice was potent in reach and sublime expression for all quarters of the audience-room,
while the rich, mellow, glowing quality of the
tone made its way to every ear, as well as to
every heart. She was enthusiastically recalled,
and repeated the aria, turning her voice and
person more directly to the chorus part of the
house, where a shower of plaudits had a signifi-
cance which could not be mistaken."

Thus closed a delightful week, full of the joy that pervaded the very air with the assurance of peace and freedom, and found its best and deepest expression in the noble voices of the singers.

CHAPTER IV.

DURING the rest of the year 1869 Adelaide remained at home, in consequence of the increasing illness of her father, sparing neither strength nor expense to give him every comfort and luxury. She had indeed devoted assistance from Arvilla and her brothers, Matilde being at the time in Europe. Towards the spring of 1870 Mr. Phillipps revived, and Adelaide, escorted by her brother Adrian, took a concert-tour in the West. By one of those chances, as they are called, which occur in life, we met her in San Francisco, and attended several concerts in which she sang, and she had a very cordial reception.

In October, 1870, Mr. Phillipps died at Marshfield. His daughter returned in time to watch over his last days with more than filial devotion.

In the ensuing winter she joined another concert troupe, going South and West. The following notice from a correspondent of the *Evening Transcript* (L. B. B.) gives evidence of her reception in New Orleans: —

"Miss Phillipps, that sterling artiste, is meeting with almost unprecedented success South and West, giving concerts in all the cities and large towns. The press of New Orleans is loud in praises of her artistic efforts in that city. One of the largest halls was engaged and filled on each occasion by that well-known musical community. Miss Phillipps will return to Boston in season for the Triennial Festival, which is to take place in May, having been engaged as principal contralto for several months. In the meantime she has other cities to visit and other conquests to make. Success attend her!"

The following March, 1871, Miss Phillipps sang in Brooklyn, New York, with the Philharmonic Society. She was the guest of Mr. and Mrs. Gordon L. Ford, at whose hospitable mansion Adelaide was ever welcome. The audience at Brooklyn was always a sympathetic one to her, and whether in opera or concerts she received their cordial reception.

On Easter Monday, 1871, Carl Rosa opened a season at the Academy of Music in New York, the principal artists being Madame Parepa Rosa, Adelaide Phillipps, Wachtel, and Santley.* We were present at the Academy on the opening night, when the house presented a most brilliant aspect. The immense crowd was, as one of the performers afterwards said to me (Mr. Santley), " almost an oppressive although very gratifying sight from the stage." The enthusiasm was contagious.

* The magnificent baritone of Mr. Santley will be remembered by all who heard the " Dolby Troupe," consisting of Mr. and Mrs. Patey, Miss Wynne, Mr. W. H. Cummings, and Mr. Santley. Their rendering of the great oratorios, as well as that of their perfectly-finished ballads, given with rare excellence, proved them to be fitly placed as first in rank among English artists.

The opera was "Il Trovatore," and as
Azucena lay apparently sleeping on the
bank, she was not as in Paris, in any danger of stage fright, but searching with
half shut eyes for our place in the audience
in order to know that we had good seats.
Having ascertained that fact, Azucena
composed herself. The tributes from the
leading New York papers at the time
were strong in their tone of appreciation
of this rare combination, of which Mr.
Rosa was the conductor. The following
extracts will give their general impression: —

"The opening of the new opera season last
night was attended with all the magnificence
which the combination effected by Mr. Rosa
seemed to require. The fact that the receipts
were about nine thousand two hundred dollars
proves that the Academy was crowded to a degree without parallel in the history of the
Academy of Music. The performance was
worthy of this excitement. Parepa Rosa,
Phillipps, Wachtel, and Santley form a cast

which cannot be surpassed. The audience thought so last night, and as each member of the great quartette appeared on the stage a hearty round of applause gave a cordial welcome. The opera was " Il Trovatore." Of Madame Rosa, who has so often sang the part of *Leonora,* it is unnecessary to speak at full length, but she sang with great power and effect. Miss Phillipps, the *Azucena* of the evening, was welcomed back with genuine warmth, and gave a nobly dramatic delineation of the gypsy mother. Her voice throughout was rich and melodious, and her action far transcended what is usually witnessed on the lyric stage. Wachtel and Santley gave us two of the most notable personations which the average opera-goer may ever hope to witness. One all fire, the other all finish."

The performances which followed were all equally successful, and the crowded audiences filled the house through the season.

Miss Phillipps said that it was almost the only instance in her experience where the demand for tickets was so great that none were at the disposal of the artists.

At the conclusion of her engagement with Mr. Rosa's troupe Miss Phillipps returned to Boston to take her place in the leading contralto *rôles* of the second Triennial Festival of the Handel and Haydn Society. These were in the oratorios of Elijah, Messiah, and Sterndale Bennett's " Woman of Samaria," and in the concerts of the week.

The tenor of the second Triennial was Mr. William H. Cummings, of London. To a pure tenor voice was added great culture and style. Mr. Cummings is a man whose whole nature and training fits him peculiarly for oratorio music, and all who listen to his rendering of the tenor *rôles* in the Elijah and the Messiah must have acknowledged that their effect was due to something beyond what was contained in the scores even of Handel and Mendelssohn. Mr. Cummings expressed great admiration of Miss Phillipps' artistic powers, especially her rendering of

the aria, "He was despised," which he said
he had never heard so effectively given.
This was the only occasion on which her
emotional nature almost overcame her
artistic training. Some chord was touched;
the listeners could not hear. She sang
through the aria perfectly, but she sank
down on her seat in tears.

For the following anecdote, which be-
longs to the time of the "Second Triennial," I am indebted to Mrs. Gordon
L. Ford, of Brooklyn, N. Y., as well as
for other appreciative expressions growing
out of her long acquaintance with Adelaide, which will be added later in the
record: —

"An instance of her sweet temper and quick
tact occurred at a rehearsal of the Handel and
Haydn Society in Boston. Mme. Rudersdorf,
who had come from London to sing at the festival, made some complaints of the inaccuracy of
the singers equal in rank to herself, with whom
she was practising. Some of them were dis-
posed to resent this criticism on the spot by

withdrawing their services; and, for a moment, the festival seemed endangered. Miss Phillipps came to the rescue, and, springing up said, in her sweet, cordial way, 'I think we all deserve that reproof; we certainly do take some of these passages in a very scrambling fashion; let us try if we cannot hit the notes at once without a scramble,' and harmony was restored by her assuming the reproof and sharing the blame.

"I never saw her imperious but once, and then she had much provocation. She was to sing 'Oh rest in the Lord!' at a Philharmonic concert. There had been no rehearsal. The audience waited for her appearance; but when the music was handed to her it had been altered from the contralto — in which it was written — to a soprano pitch, and, of course, was out of the range of Miss Phillipps' voice. She explained to the conductor, but he said he had no other scores for the orchestra. Some sharp words followed, when Mr. Richard Hoffman, the pianist, stepped forward and volunteered to play the accompaniment as Mendelssohn had written it, which was successfully done. This was the only time I ever saw her temper ruffled, and, indeed, in her stage relations with other singers she was always large-hearted, kindly, and forbearing in word and deed."

In the third Triennial of the Boston
Handel and Haydn Society, in 1874, Miss
Phillipps took the contralto *rôles* in J. K.
Paine's oratorio of " St. Peter," and in
Bach's " Passion Music," both works
demanding much study and practice.
Bach's Passion music had been given in
selections in 1871, but was now presented
more fully. Miss Phillipps studied the
difficult scores most earnestly, and her
rendering of it was entirely appreciated
by the critics. In 1881, when the directors of the Boston Handel and Haydn
Society were obliged to turn, almost at the
last moment, in their utmost need to
Matilde Phillipps for the contralto *rôles*
of the Passion music, Adelaide was very
ill, but she rose at once to her artistic
power; and lying on her couch heard her
sister's rendering of the part. Matilde
had sang the *rôle* previously, but several
years had passed, and to recall such difficult music at so brief a notice required

both courage and sympathy. Adelaide was entirely gratified by the favorable report of her sister's performance. Miss Phillipps' last appearance with the Handel and Haydn Society was November 24, 1878, and, as we now know, closed appropriately with Verdi's " Requiem Mass."

A quartette company was organized by Miss Phillipps in 1874, with which she visited various States in the Union. Perhaps a letter received during this tour will give a glimpse of the work of such an undertaking: —

ST. PAUL, Nov. 9, 1874.

DEAR MRS. WATERSTON, — This is such a beautiful place I wish you were here with me to enjoy it. We have had a very successful trip thus far ; very fine weather, and the performances go well and the public are pleased. The expenses are greater than I expected; sometimes three hundred dollars more than I thought, but as yet the payments are all right. My tenor, Mr. Karl, has a beautiful voice, sings well, and is handsome, which pleases the ladies. So far so good. The baritone, Orlandini, has a fine voice and is a good artist, as is also the buffo, Barcelli, We only meet at the theatre and in the cars. They all seem contented.

Etta Newcomb is with me, and is a great comfort. We manage to take a walk almost every day, so I am not tired yet. We have been through Kansas, out to Omaha, Dubuque, Winona, and hurried here on Sunday morning. After the concert of Winona we slept one hour, leaving the hotel at half-past twelve o'clock. Poor Etta, I woke her singing, " Oh, an artist's life for me!" She understands the pleasures of it now! We shall be here two nights; then into Michigan and Illinois; Chicago on Monday and Tuesday; St. Catherine's, Canada, Friday; Rochester, N. Y., Monday; back to Massachusetts and New Hampshire. After that I do not know where we go; work back West I suppose. I gave up Boston in November as too early. I shall try to arrange for February. I hope your visit to the mountains was pleasant. Let me hear from you at Chicago.

Yours, always,

ADELAIDE.

A scrap from another letter written in the country, somewhere in New England, gives a pretty picture: "I am in a nice farm-house, sitting in a kitchen with a great open fire. Its light glances on knitting-needles and gold beads. It is all very quaint and pleasant. They are such nice good people. I sang to them, and though I have had larger audiences, few, I think, who enjoyed the songs more."

A larger organization, under the title of the Adelaide Phillipps Opera Company, of which she was the manager, visited various parts of the country. It was a double company, and included among its members some of those artists mentioned in the letter from St. Paul, with many additions. Miss Colville, Adelaide, and Matilde Phillipps were the prima donnas.

With this company she went through the South and West, and was certainly very successful according to all the reports of the newspapers in the various places visited. But she found the care and responsibility too great for a woman who was also one of the artists. The expenses were very heavy, and the management of so large a company difficult. When the season closed it was not a financial success, for Miss Phillipps paid all debts, just and unjust, being highly conscientious, which very few managers would aspire to be considered.

Matilde Phillipps, who had been singing in opera in Sardinia, left the favorable opening there, and returned to America to aid her sister in this undertaking. Matilde made her first appearance in New York. A note from her contains these heartfelt words: "Do you know that Adelaide took a small part in the opera of *Ceneratula* at my début. As my success increased her delight was so great that she forgot to be the cruel sister Tisbie, and became the noble-hearted Adelaide, showing all her pleasure in the expression of her face so beaming and true."

Singers are not exempt from embarrassing accidents, as was told by Adelaide on her return from a concert in a country town. "I had packed my dress," said she, "in a champagne basket, and tied it up with green ribbons. We arrived in good season, and after tea I retired to my room to make my toilet rather leisurely, as is my wont. By-and-by I thought I would take out my dress, which was a very pretty one. So I untied my green ribbons and opened the champagne basket. Imagine my feelings on beholding a pair of high boots, rough coat, and all the rest of a man's habiliments. My charming dress, lace, flowers, and all the rest of the finery had fallen into the hands of some man, who by a wonderful coincidence, had packed up *his* clothes in a champagne basket and tied it with green ribbons! Neither of us could avail ourselves of each other's garments. It was too late to make any other preparation than to brush up my travelling dress, add the few additional ornaments I had brought in my pocket, and send on word to the audience that Miss Phillipps regretted extremely that her evening dress had not arrived in time, which was certainly true. I really felt for their disappointment, for, however well we sing, all goes better when we are handsomely dressed; and I fear they felt defrauded of half the price of their tickets. They were very good, however, and applauded me and my black silk." "What became of your dress?" was the feminine exclamation. "Oh, it was found. The man was glad to get his boots again."

Of the many concerts at which she appeared it is impossible to make any record. No one who heard her songs, whether gay or pathetic, can fail to recall the varied chords she touched in the human soul. Her ringing laugh in a frolicsome *jeu d'esprit*, the words of which were written by Miss Kate Field, set to music by Bendalari, contrasted with songs that stirred our hearts. All must remember, whether heard at home or from the concert platform, her rendering of "Auld Robin Gray" and "Kathleen Mavourneen." Another charming *chanson*, "The Danube River," still flows like the stream it pictured through the memory. A western paper, the Indianapolis *Sentinel*, thus graphically describes some of Miss Phillipps' songs: " Between the acts of 'Martha,' in response to the uproarious *encore* of ' The Laughing Song,' Miss Phillipps sang the ' Rosebush' (an epitome of woman's life), a ballad which must have been written to suit the wonderful pathos, passion, and sensibility of her ripe and mellow voice. Her perfect enunciation of every word made them plain to the remotest auditor, and were received with breathless silence. She threw a world of sentiment into every line, but her power was conspicuously displayed in rendering the tender couplet —

> " ' She pressed her hand to her throbbing breast,
> With love's first wonderful rapture blest.'

" And the sadly suggestive refrain —

> " ' Withered and dead they fall to the ground,
> And silently cover a new-made mound.'

"Miss Phillipps' versatility was displayed by a quiet transition from tears to smiles when she responded to a third *encore*, with ' Coming through the Rye,' the bloom of which is perennial."

As these words recall those songs, how many will catch their echo in their own hearts out of the silence which now rests upon her lips. During a summer which succeeded a fatiguing season, Miss Phillipps, in company with Miss Kate Field, went to Europe. The voyage was always a pleasure to Adelaide, and to all her fellow-passengers who were able to enjoy her society.

She visited the Pyrenees, and made various excursions. In London Adelaide called upon Madame Parepa Rosa at her pleasant home, surrounded by every comfort and elegance. The additional happiness then anticipated was, alas! never realized; and in a few months the mother and child left the world together. Mme. Parepa Rosa's death was sincerely mourned in America, where she had many friends. The voices of Mme. Rosa and Miss Phillipps so often had mingled in oratorio and opera, that to unite their names together now seems, in memory of all we owe to their gifts, but a fitting homage to two grand artistes.

In 1879 Miss Phillipps joined the Ideal Opera Company, under the direction of Miss E. H. Ober, and carried into it her vocal and dramatic culture and her unflagging spirit. She continued attached to that company until December, 1881, when she made her last appearance on the stage in Cincinnati.

These sketches of Miss Phillipps' professional work suggest somewhat of their
variety and extent; but the real experience of an artist is faintly outlined by any
enumeration of *rôles*, or reports of success or applause.   In such a career much
is required; serious thought, hard study,
anxious hours; the fatigue from travelling
hundreds of miles before taking a difficult
part, leaving the opera when over at mid-
night for the next city; this is but part of
the regular routine.   Added to these trials
come exactions of managers, jealousy of
rivals, uncertainty of remuneration after
the toils of the season are over.   There
are many ways by which the prosperous
path of a popular artist may be circum-
vented without the facts appearing openly;
not to mention the varying phases of the
capricious public, and always being at the
mercy of newspaper reporters.   Many of
these trials await all artists whose profession brings them before the public, be it

on canvas or in marble; but especially is
it true of the musician, and eminently of
the lyric artist, whose success or defeat
may depend on one supreme moment.
To most people who go to the drama or
opera the actors or singers are mere appearances who come out to amuse us, and
we think them rewarded by applause and
flowers. So they are, in a degree. But
how little do we consider what they have
gone through in a life-long preparation to
give us an evening's amusement. Few
realize what is required of a dramatic, and
yet more of an operatic artist. The memory, the musical ear, the words of a foreign language, the action of the part, be it
tragic or comic, presence of mind to meet
all emergencies without a sign of disturb-
ance, even when painful accidents occur,
or life itself is in danger. Sometimes the
performer is suffering physical pain, or
from recent illness, often in great personal
anxiety or heavy bereavement, yet they

must come before the public and play their part before critics who make no allowances : —

"Watch the part of the player bravely and deftly
    done,
See the difficult height attained, the loud applauses
    won,
Weep with his passionate sorrow, thrill with his pas-
    sionate bliss,
Blending your joyous laughter with that happy laugh
    of his,
Well that his marvellous acting, dazzles, wins, refines,
Who thinks of the desperate effort written between
    the lines ? "

Miss Phillipps was not one of those who decried her profession. The stage was as familiar to her as her home, and she always maintained that men and women were not misled by being connected with it, any further than their characteristic tendencies would have been shown in the temptations and trials of life in whatever sphere they moved.

"The actual work behind the scenes," she would say, "leaves no time for those sort of things people imagine; we are too busy, often too anxious, to attend to anything but our parts. The heroes and heroines of the opera are seldom the lovers they enact, often quite the reverse."

The bare rafters, the coarsely-painted scenes, the workmen in their shirt-sleeves, the cold draughts sweeping through the comfortless passageways, suggest only work and risk of health to any one who, stepping across the line, sees the reality instead of the appearance.

Miss Phillipps was eminently of the Italian school of vocal music, the school of nearly all the great singers of the past. Since she first appeared on the lyric stage changes have come over the musical world. The great German composers are more widely known, and Italian opera is waning.

Long since Miss Phillipps' career began the opera bouffe has introduced its demoralizing influence on the stage and on society. French dramas have instilled their poisonous atmosphere, all the more dangerous because imbibed through the medium of grace and talent.

As changes await every human invention, let us hope that this age of sensationalism may pass away, bringing a better taste to the community.

Had Miss Phillipps first appeared in America, her talents as an actress and vocalist duly stamped by European fame, she would doubtless have received a greater ovation. The proverb, "A prophet is not without honor save in his own country," cannot justly be said to have been verified in her experience; yet it is doubtless true she was too near the daily life of the country, especially that of the city of her adoption, to become that mysterious idol, a foreign prima donna.

If Adelaide Phillipps had thrown herself entirely into her profession, without regard to any motive but selfish success, she would doubtless have filled a wider space in the operatic world, and taken her place as one of the great artistes of her time. But she never swerved from the straight and narrow way in which she walked as a woman. That she sacrificed worldly prosperity to principle, and after a long life of great and generous exertion left but a modest fortune, is certainly true. Although a conscientious artiste, and entering with interest into the duties of her profession, her heart was in her personal life, her home, and with those friends whom she loved.

A sacred voice has said "no man can serve two masters; ye cannot serve God and Mammon." Adelaide made her choice, and it was not Mammon.

CHAPTER V.

A FARM in Marshfield was purchased in 1860 for Mr. Alfred Phillipps, the eldest brother of the family; there they removed, and it became their home. It was a valuable farm, near the sea, and adjacent to the estate of Daniel Webster. This home was the centre of Miss Phillipps' thoughts and interests. Here she returned every summer, when not professionally engaged, to enjoy country life. Perhaps the following letter, written to my sister after a visit to Marshfield, will best show the life led there:—

"JUNE, '74.

"I met Adelaide at the station in Boston and arrived safely at Marshfield, where four of the family dogs received her with great emotion,—two great Newfoundlanders, 'Cæsar' and 'Lyon,' a beautiful brown setter, and a funny little Es-

HOME AT MARSHFIELD.

quimaux terrier, 'Tasso,' the principal actors. When we reached the house poor old Rip, the aged bloodhound, who has figured in many of Adelaide's dog-stories (since she brought him in a basket, a young puppy, from Havana), could only look pathetically in her face and feebly wag his tail. The house, where we were received by Arvilla, is very pleasant and homelike, and seemed gay with young people coming and going. Altogether it was like a family in a story-book, with varied histories and prima donnas among them, and somewhat like living in a Landseer picture of dogs, with humans thrown in; humans, however, who possessed many talents and musical ability. We walked to the beach the first day, about a mile from the house, accompanied by four of the dogs. On our way an imprudent woodchuck was killed by 'Lyon'; it was an unlucky day for that woodchuck. The farm is under cultivation, Mr. Alfred and his brother Edwin having charge of it. Mr. Alfred Phillipps also has a conservatory, where he raises flowers for the city as well as home. Near the house is a statue of a female figure looking downwards. This was placed there when the Thomas family, whose ancestors owned the place, met in commemoration of the first settlers of Marshfield. The figure holds an inverted

vase in her left hand, and in her right, which
also clasps her dress, a wreath. The design
idealises the return of their ancestress, Sarah
Pitney Thomas, to the spot where she came as
a bride December 2, 1648. Mrs. Thomas was
an heroic woman, who grew up in the wilder-
ness, bravely facing its dangers and maintaining
through life that unswerving faith which was
the characteristic of the Pilgrim mothers. With
a sincere, but perhaps fanciful, intention, the
wreath in the hand of the figure typifies a gift
and recognition from the spirit of the true
woman of two centuries ago to the true woman
now mistress of the old Thomas homestead.
The depression in the ground which marks the
cellar of the first home of Mrs. Thomas, and
above which she bends, is filled with flowers. I
was, indeed, on the sacred sod first trodden by
our New England fathers. The low-lying hills,
the ocean view, were the same to-day as when
they looked upon them, and must have recalled
their native land, amid the cares, the sufferings
and efforts of which we, with little thought of
them, now reap the harvest.

"The next afternoon we visited the house which
belonged to Daniel Webster. You will remember our visit there many years ago, with our
mother, when I was a child. That part of the

estate then belonged to the Thomas family, although Mr. Webster had already made it his head-
quarters for fishing excursions. The great elm
still lives, and is a magnificent tree. The house
has been entirely altered, and the part added by
Mr. Webster changes its aspect. The propor-
tions of the library are ample and dignified:
here many rare books, pictures, and other gifts
presented to Mr. Webster are gathered. Mrs.
Fletcher Webster kindly showed me every object of interest, and took me over the house,
which she has done all in her power to preserve.
It is impressive, for it still seems to hold the
history of a very remarkable man; but a sphere
of melancholy pervades the whole mansion. The
rain, which began to fall heavily, prevented us
from seeing the grounds or visiting the sea-
shore, where Mr. Thomas first met Mr. Webster
and mistook him for some strange fisherman.
'Why, Mrs. Quincy,' he said to our mother, 'I
never had seen such a fisherman before; he had
great boots and old clothes, but yet he had such
eyes. He came home with me, and that was
the beginning of his making this house a sort of
home.'

" The next day, the rain ceasing, Adelaide
drove with me to Duxbury along the pathway of
our Pilgrim fathers. 'The bay where the May-

flower lay' was in the distance, and we passed
the French Cable Telegraph Station, between
which two points of progress a vast history lies.
It was Sunday afternoon, and as we drove through
Duxbury all was quiet.   Here many retired sea-
captains live in supernaturally neat houses, with
cheerful grounds full of flowers, giving one a
pleasant sense of rest after storms.   We drove
to "Captain's hill," where a monument to Miles
Standish was commenced in 1872.   At the lay-
ing of the corner-stone a large number of ladies
and gentlemen attended.   In a manuscript note
to the pamphlet containing an account of the
proceedings, by Mr. Stephen M. Allen, corre-
sponding secretary of the Standish Monument
Association, he writes: 'As a matter of courtesy
General Horace Binney Sargent, president of
the association, handed the spade to the ladies
first, and in their behalf Miss Adelaide Phillipps
took it, and turned the first sod for the founda-
tion of the monument.'

"The evenings of my pleasant visit were
varied by music.   Suddenly Adelaide exclaimed,
"You must hear Cæsar sing."   Accordingly
the black Newfoundlander, of whose vocal powers I had heard frequently, was led to the
piano, and sat looking up gravely in Adelaide's
face, who began to play an accompaniment.

"Sing, Cæsar, sing," she cried; and, aided by her voice, Cæsar certainly uttered sounds of more or less musical effect, somewhat mournful, it must be confessed, yet greatly to the pleasure of his affectionate friend, while Cæsar took our applause with great dignity. The close of my visit was somewhat saddened by the death of poor old Rip, which took place in the afternoon on our return from Duxbury. Adelaide had loved him well for fourteen years, and mourned over him, though glad that his sufferings from that incurable disease, old age, were over. Adelaide superintended his burial in a quiet spot, which she will tenderly guard. The event was rather sad; and, to show the uncertainties of life on a farm, one of Arvilla's favorite ducklings departed for duckling paradise, at the same time poor old Rip died.

"My pleasant visit closing, I took leave of Adelaide, and was escorted home by Mr. Adrian Phillipps."

In recalling the pleasant excursions we made together, a few days which Adelaide and I spent with Mr. and Mrs. Eben Dale, at their beautiful residence in Gloucester, Massachusetts, comes back with great

interest. Mr. and Mrs. Dale had been
for many years her true friends. Their
brother, Mr. Theron Dale, has been already named as one of the musical company who met at Mme. Arnoult's house,
when Adelaide was preparing for the lyric
stage. At the time of our Gloucester visit,
Mr. Theron Dale and his sister, Mrs. Swett,
occupied the old homestead in the town,
while his brother's mansion stood near
the sea, where the waves broke upon a
small beach below the cliff on which the
house stood. We were most hospitably
entertained at both houses, enjoyed delightful drives, and the evenings were
filled with music. Mr. Theron Dale was
a very musical man, sang well, and im-
provised gracefully on the piano. He was
much and generously interested in church
music and all connected with the subject.
Few are left who enjoyed those days
together. The master of the house, his
brother Theron, Mr. Turnbull, the son-in-

law, his lovely daughter, then a little
child, and now Adelaide, have passed behind the veil which is so thin and yet so
strong.

Adelaide's generous interest in young
people was often manifested among her
neighbors. It was her custom to invite the
young ladies of Duxbury in the summer
to what she called " an orchard party."
A table was placed under the trees,
ornamented with flowers, and on it arranged the delicacies of a five-o'clock
tea; Adelaide, her sisters and the brothers, waiting upon the company. When
the evening came all adjourned to the
house, and finished the visit with music
and dancing. A new hall having been
built for the Marshfield Agricultural and
Horticultural Society, the expense ex-
ceeded, as is often the case, the calcula-
tions for the enterprise; Miss Phillipps
offered to give a concert in aid of the
fund, and gathered about her a number

of professional friends to aid in the concert. Her sister Matilde having returned
home, was also enlisted. In order to make
it more attractive, a scene from "Cinderella" was introduced, for which the
young ladies of the "orchard-party"
were trained as chorus, Matilde taking
the part of Cinderella. When the time
for the representation came the whole
neighborhood turned out, many of the
older Old Colony people never having
heard a concert or an opera. The success was great, both artistically and
financially. So grateful were the recipients
of Miss Phillipps' generosity that the
members of the Agricultural Society
wished to give a concert in her honor.
This offer she decidedly declined for
herself, but finding that her refusal gave
much disappointment, she consented that
the tribute should be transferred to her
sister Matilde, who was commencing
her professional career. This was ac-

cordingly done. About this time Mrs. Livermore made a Temperance address at the Agricultural Hall in Marshfield. Miss Phillipps went to hear the gifted speaker. The earnest, graphic address moved her very much. At the close she expressed her interest and sympathy. " Let me ask you," she said, " to go home with me — all my singers are at my house to-day arranging concerts for the next season. I ran away from work and them to hear you." Mrs. Livermore accepted the invitation, and enjoyed a concert of rare sweetness and beauty. " It must be our best," said Miss Phillips, " for the woman to whom we sing is not only ' one of a thousand, but is more than a thousand.'" At the close she said, "Now, Mrs. Livermore, when I can serve you for this object with my voice, command me. There must surely be occasions on which I can do something to aid in this ' woman's temperance work.'"

Mrs. Livermore promised to call on her when free from professional engage-- ments, but the time never came.

Among the friends of Miss Phillipps residing in the Old Colony were the Thaxter family, and Mr. John Quincy Thaxter had become her man of business. He was often a visitor at Marshfield, as an intimate friend of the family. On one occasion he was to spend a few days with them. The last evening of his visit closed with a gay tea-party, at which all seemed especially happy. As he rose from the table, he said, " do you know we are thirteen? I wonder which it will be." The answer soon came. The next day Mr. Thaxter went to Boston, and on his return a severe accident happened to the railroad car. He had stepped upon the platform as it neared Hingham, to greet in pass- ing two relatives, who always looked for him at that hour. He was thrown from the car and instantly killed. This was a very severe shock to all connected with him, especially to Miss Phillipps, whose ready sympathy for Mr. Thaxter's family, as well as her own loss of a true friend, was strongly felt. I remember the pathetic tones in which she related to me what had happened, and dwelt sorrowfully on her visit to his parents, whose grief she shared. "His mother asked me never to forget how he enjoyed my singing, and added, 'When you can will you sing something he loved, in the evening about the time he died?'"

The loss of Mr. Thaxter was serious in several ways to Miss Phillipps, for, cut off in a moment as he was, some of her investments were not entirely arranged; as usual, however, she had not much thought for herself. After this event Miss Phillipps placed her business affairs in the hands of Mr. Samuel S. Shaw, who remained a true guardian of all her interests to the close of her life, and whose sincere attention to her welfare and that of her family remains unbroken.

From the description given of Miss Phillipps' home life, it will be clearly understood how happy it was. Her interest in the farm and all the arrangements of her brother Alfred may perhaps be better told in a few letters written when away from Marshfield on professional tours. Mr. Alfred Phillipps was specially interested in horticulture, and received very strong tributes from the horticultural societies of the Old Colony for his taste and skill in floral designs which ornamented their annual agricultural and horticultural fairs. From the following letters it is evident how her thoughts ever turned to Marshfield, —

"DEAR ALFRED, — What is this pretty flower I send you? It was in a basket given me last night. You ought to have some like it. We are very successful. Do not overwork yourself.

Be sure and have the asparagus-bed attended to at once."

In another letter, dated from Chicago, she writes, —

"I hope all is going well with you. We are doing finely here. Please have plenty of melon seeds planted. Have you had the grafts of the black apple-trees attended to? I hope so. Do not forget about the road. If they make it straight, and take away the curve round our house, I shall never feel like seeing Marshfield again. Let me hear about it. How are all the flowers?

"Your affectionate sister,

"ADELAIDE."

The following note testifies that Miss Phillipps' interest in young ladies was not confined to "orchard-parties" at Marsh-field, —

"HOTEL PELHAM, BOSTON, May 18, 1881.

"DEAR ALFRED, — I intend giving a tea to the young ladies of our chorus, about twelve or fourteen. It is to come off after the matinee. Can you let me have some flowers? I should like enough to make little bouquets, putting them together in the centre of the table in a mass;

when the young ladies leave, it can be taken apart, and each receive a bouquet; so you understand they must be small.   I shall want the bag of silver, and a table-cloth long enough for ten or twelve people. Emily will attend to that. Are you having any lobsters yet down with you ? If so, I should like some, quite fresh.   I think you and Edwin had better come up on Saturday, as I do not like trusting the silver to a stranger. Let me know if I can depend on you ; also about the lobsters. We give the ' Chimes of Normandy' at the matinee ; so I shall have tea at half-past five o'clock, as the young ladies sing again in the evening.   I shall run down to Marshfield on Monday afternoon, and the architect will come on Tuesday, so I hope the cellar is in good order.   Love to Edwin and yourself.
                    " From your
                              " ADELAIDE."

Those who remember Miss Phillipps' charming representation that afternoon in the " Chimes of Normandy," and the exquisite duet between Mr. Karl and herself, could hardly have believed the heroine of that tender passage was " on hospitable thoughts intent."

"BURNETT HOUSE, CINCINNATI, Dec. 30, 1881.

"DEAR ALFRED, — I wish you all a happy New Year. Do you know you wrote me a very good letter? I enjoyed it much. Write me again when you have time. I am so glad to hear about the services at the river. Miss Devereux has indeed done a good work. What did you do at Christmas? Did any one dine with you? Do you send flowers to Boston? Be sure and remind Mr. Pierce of his promise to go down to Marshfield, and have the dining-room chimney made all right. I shall run down to Marshfield when I am singing in Boston, and make arrangements about the chimney-piece. We are doing a fine business here. We shall be in Pittsburg next week, then in Baltimore, then in Philadelphia two weeks. I wish you would ask Edwin to make me two trellises, rustic work. Miss Cowing is going to give me a honeysuckle, and I want one for that to put near the clematis ; it is such a mean thing the clematis is on now.

"Love to all.

"ADELAIDE."

The services at the river, mentioned in the preceding letter, were arranged for the benefit of a small fishing village

called Green Harbor, in Marshfield. Miss
Devereaux was principally instrumental in
making this effort for the religious benefit
of the place. Services were first held in
a cottage, but Miss Devereaux's zeal enlisted others, and a small church has since
been erected, which is now well attended.

Even in Carlsbad, when fatal sickness
was upon her, Marshfield was ever near
her heart. In one of those revivals of
physical strength, which often precede
the close of life, Adelaide writes thus to
Alfred, — the last letter the brother was
ever to receive from her hand: —

> " KÖNIGS VILLA, CARLSBAD,
>   September 14, 1882.

"DEAR ALFRED, — I am getting on quite
well, and hope to return next summer.

" Now I want you to prepare me a nice piece of
land up near the house, which will be my vegetable garden—Adelaide's garden. It must be large
enough for a strawberry-bed. Please to plant
plenty of melons, early vegetable, etc., etc. It
must be near the barn, so that I can have the
water turned there if necessary. Now do this

for me, there's a good fellow. Prepare it this fall, and some time I will fence it in. Have you got those grapes planted yet, like Dr. Henry's? I hope you are not troubling yourself about the fair; it takes up too much of your time when you are attending to your greenhouse. Now be sure and get in your plants early; do not leave it late. Save the geraniums. The people here and all over Europe are suffering from wet weather; rain, rain, rain. I hope you will write me a nice Marshfield letter, telling me all the news. Give my love to Emily. Love to all.

"Yours affectionately,

"ADELAIDE."

The "Emily" so frequently mentioned is a faithful domestic, who sometimes accompanied Adelaide on her professional tours, but generally superintended the household at Marshfield. An invaluable friend is such a member of any family; true to their interests and devoted to their comfort in sickness or in health, and who in this instance has for twenty years shared their joys and their sorrows. Such a

helper and friend the family possessed in
"Emily," who remains to cheer those
who, like herself, have met with an
irreparable loss in their beloved Adelaide.

In Miss Phillipps' domestic life, as well
as among her friends, the charm of her
magnetic presence came with light and
warmth. I can even now seem to hear
that light, firm step as she approaches
the door of the favorite room where this
tribute is written, raising gayly a peculiar
note known to us both as heralding her
approach, and her cordial response to the
greeting, "Come rest your weary little
feet at a friend's threshold."

The home at Marshfield was the centre
of Adelaide Phillipps' interests and affections; to it she dedicated a large pro-
portion of the results of her untiring efforts
in her profession. Her devotion to her
family has often been mentioned as "a
burden" upon her; this idea she always

resented. "What should I do it for if not for them?" she said, with feeling.

The record of Adelaide's life shows how the filial and fraternal affections and duties were its leading motive. It is not to be supposed that with all her qualities and attractions she was not sought by those who would gladly have gained the prize of such a heart, and limited its affections to what is called the nearest relation. But she resolutely turned from such suggestions. "While I am on the stage," she said, "I shall never marry. It was a determination I made early in my life, and I have seen no reason to regret it."

To make her home all that she wished it to be for those she loved, as well as for the reception of her many friends, her expenditures may be said to have been lavish. She was never happier than when keeping open house in the summer; and those who availed themselves of her cordial invitations — and they were many —

cannot but retain a grateful recollection of her hospitalities as a hostess.

Among the enjoyments of Adelaide's life few were greater than her visits to the family of Judge Monell, at their charming residence at Fishkill-on-the-Hudson. Mrs. Monell in a letter recently received says:—

"Mr. Monell and our daughter made Miss Phillipps' acquaintance during a journey to California, and on visiting us after her return she became at once a cherished guest and friend whose coming was hailed ever after as an occasion of rejoicing. She went with us one summer to Lake Placid, in the Adirondacks, where she seemed to assimilate with the sylvan spirit of the forests and lakes of that region, saying that she never found any atmosphere where her voice flowed with such ease and pleasure to herself as among those wild scenes of the primeval forest. She did not wish to sing in any public way at the hotel, but one day she was discovered in the kitchen in the midst of the landlord's family and the guides, who were all in tears at her touching musical recital of 'Auld Robin Gray' for their especial benefit and enjoyment.

"We had the pleasure of passing a few days

at her home at Marshfield, and shall always
remember the spirit and kindness of manner by
which she enhanced our enjoyments there, our
ride to the beach in the country wagon, and our
picnic in a rustic house she had built on the
shore, where she had a curious collection of
china, of a marine and sailor-like description,
kept for that especial purpose."

In Mrs. Monell's letter she also alludes
to what Adelaide called her "sentimental
tea-set," many of her friends having con-
tributed a cup and saucer to it; and I
recall the almost childlike delight with
which she received our donations to this
peculiarly constituted "sentimental" collection.

There was as great a versatility of
power in her private life as in her professional work. She threw herself into
the experiences of her friends without any
effort; we never felt she was *trying* to
love or sympathize with us. In a visit
from her, many years ago, after our return
from Europe, where a great bereavement

had befallen us, Adelaide's presence was a soothing one. At the time she was one of an opera company giving performances every evening. The newspapers, and the reports of our friends, were full of her praises, especially in her gayest *rôles*. From these she would come home, pleased to bring me the flowers that the audience had showered upon her, and change quietly from the playful character with which at that moment people were associating her, to the tender friend.

An extract from a letter written by Miss Mary G. Monell touches upon the same quality in Adelaide's character:—

"All her friends must have felt her deep and intense sympathy in the sorrows of others, and the quick and beautiful way in which she expressed it. I remember once, in the earlier days of our friendship, the sudden death of a dear friend darkened my life. Adelaide was in Boston, and seeing a notice of the death in the papers, started at once and came to us. Without warning she walked quietly into my room, saying simply, 'My dear, I have come to help, if I can. Shall I stay?' Need I say she did stay, and then took me with her to Marshfield, where her keen sympathy and constant care did more than all else to keep morbidness away."

No morbid tendency belonged to her healthy nature. Times of depression indeed, came, owing to the circumstances in which she was placed at the moment, but she threw off despondency quickly. Notwithstanding the buoyancy of her spirits, and the energy she possessed, she had in her constitution a reluctance to action. After a few days of entire rest, she would say, as she gathered herself up to plunge into busy life again, " How lazy I should be if I had not been obliged to work ! "

Mrs. Gordon L. Ford, at whose home in Brooklyn, N. Y., Adelaide was a welcome guest, recognizes this element in her nature: —

" I think her life alternated beween pe-
riods of rest and effort, and she gathered
strength for her severe labors by intervals
of entire passivity. I have even heard
her called indolent, but her energy far
overbalanced any inborn tendency to
lethargy, and was unceasing and untiring
when anything remained to be done. She
had strong social feeling and social talent,
and made the joys and sorrows of her
friends her own; yet nothing could keep
her from her engagements, and her work-
ing career was characterized by patience,
enthusiasm and conscience, which, added
to her natural gifts, carried her to the top
of her profession. It sometimes seemed
to me that, as she combined many opposite traits of character, she must have had
ancestors of various races, and different
strains of blood must have met in her;
for she had the firmness of purpose, per-
sistency of will, and strong sense of duty
and affection that pervade the northern

nations, and at the same time possessed
the quick emotions and the versatile genius
of the Latin races.   The public knew and
appreciated the artist; her friends loved
and trusted the woman, who was essen-
tially what the Italians call *simpatica*.
Her voice showed this sympathetic quality, and in its natural *timbre* melted the
soul; for while she excelled in florid execution, there was a deep undertone in it
of strength, of humanity, which was the
keynote of her character."

The allusion Mrs. Ford makes to Adelaide's social talents and tastes is verified
by the experiences of all her friends.
Had her lot been so cast, she would have
been a brilliant "woman of society." As
a *raconteur* she had a wonderful gift and
much power of mimicry.   To these qualities was added the ease with which she
spoke several foreign languages.   She
never used her conversational powers to
the disadvantage of others, passing deftly

over the characters of those whose con-
duct towards herself, personally or professionally, merited severe censure.
Sincere in her friendships, forgiving to
her detractors, generous almost to a fault
towards any whom she could aid, her unconscious rectitude bore her on through
life, without its ever occurring to her that
such a course was at all remarkable.

CHAPTER VI.

WHILE engaged in professional work with the Ideal Opera Company, during the winter of 1880, Miss Phillipps had a severe attack of illness in New York, at the house of Mrs. Reed. This kind friend's tender care doubtless prolonged her life. In consequence of her illness her brother, Dr. Frederic Phillipps, was summoned from San Francisco to attend her, but on arrival was so ill himself as to be unable to remain near her. His sister, urged doubtless by this fact, seemed to rally all the forces of her nature to meet the emergency. She soon left New York and came home to make arrangements for the comfort of her brother. Marshfield was too distant for her visits to him; she therefore took a furnished house, then

vacant, belonging to her friends, Mr. and
Mrs. J. Henry Sears, and removed her
brother and some members of the Marshfield household to the pleasant mansion in
Dorchester, associated in her mind with
many recollections.   Miss Phillipps made
the acquaintance of Mr. Sears on one of
her voyages, and from that time both Mr.
and Mrs. Sears had been true and appreciative friends, whose home she often
had shared in her many transits from
one place to another.   Dr. Phillipps
had held for several years the appoint-
ment of surgeon at the hospital at
Aspinwall, Panama; afterwards took the
position of surgeon on board one of the
great steamships plying between San
Francisco, Japan and China.   The fre-
quent attacks of Panama fever, contracted
at Aspinwall, undermined his constitution,
and he came home fatally ill.   His sister
supplied every comfort.   Matilde, Mr. and
Mrs. Adrian Phillipps, together with the

members of the family from Marshfield, were devoted nurses, Adelaide returning whenever it was possible to watch over him. At last the end came. His sister was on the stage when the telegram arrived, and was informed of the event as soon as the performance was over. The last service was held in the house at Dorchester, where many friends assembled. Adelaide showed me a beautiful wreath of white flowers sent by the "young ladies of the chorus." "You see, it is a broken one," said she. It was typical of the first break among the brothers and sisters, so long tenderly united. When all was over I said to her, "When do you return to your work?" "To-morrow," was her reply. "To-morrow?" I said, looking at her sad countenance and deep mourning dress. "Yes, I must, and there is a great deal of help in that word, 'must.'"

She resumed her place in the company under Miss Ober's direction, and continued her work for several months. It must have been near this period that her last visit to Fishkill-on-the-Hudson was made, so tenderly described by her friend, Miss Monell:

"The last time Adelaide was with us her illness and the death of her brother, though happening some months before, made her very sad. Added to this were other anxieties, which made work a necessity, so that our long talks were tinged with sadness that seemed almost prophetic. She was reluctant to leave us, and as she stood in the hall waiting for the carriage, her tears fell fast on the head of a great dog she was very fond of, and who was her constant companion when she was here. She stood talking to him in her peculiar way, while he eyed her wistfully, and then she suddenly said, 'Oh, old fellow, you understand it all, don't you; but you can't say it? Shall I sing it for you?' Taking him by the ear, she went to the

piano, seated herself, with the dog standing by her, and sang that beautiful Spanish
'Lament' that all who knew her often
heard her sing.   Her voice welled forth
and filled the house with its glorious rich-
ness, expressing all the indefinite sadness
we had felt so keenly, and something
stronger and deeper, that now seems a
foreshadowing of the long parting, for the
'Lament' was the last song she ever sang
for me; and when it was finished she
drove away through the sunlight, and
never came back again.   The picture of
her as she sat at the piano, the deep feeling and sorrow shining in her eyes, and
the great dog watching her with earnest,
questioning looks, is so deeply fixed in my
memory, it rises before me whenever I
enter the room."

A letter from my niece, Mrs. B. A.
Gould, contains a few words which,
although referring to an early period in
Adelaide's life, seem to follow fittingly

the tender memories of a later date contained in Miss Monell's letter: —

CORDOBA, S. A., November 29, 1882.

I cannot tell you how much I have felt in
seeing a day or two ago the announcement of
the death of Adelaide Phillipps.   It seems like
a part of my own life and youth gone into ever-
lasting silence.   She is one of my earliest recollections, when at eight or nine years of age I went
to see her at the old Museum.   Then came the
days when she began to sing in " Aladdin " and
" Cinderella."   Afterward we were taking lessons of Mme. Arnoult together.   Oh, how the
old days rise up before me now !   The first time
she was to sing at a concert in Boston I remember the intense interest of Madame Arnoult in
her dress, down to the rosettes on her slippers.
There was a bunch of geraniums which had been
made for me, and I think it was for that evening Mme. Arnoult asked for them to give the
one touch needed to her white dress.   She sang
Fac ut portem admirably.   In her long career
since we have met at intervals, and always, I
think, with a sense of sympathy.   I was deeply
pained to see that she is gone.   How was it
that she should lose her health in the very vigor
of life ?   Though I saw her so seldom the world
seems poorer to me without her."

The interest of Madame Arnoult in Adelaide only ceased with her own life. That expression, so common, is a very inadequate one, for we should look upon life and love as only entering into higher and purer realities and growing immortally truer and stronger. The lovely Claire Arnoult passed out of this world early in life, and her mother did not survive her many years. Her last bequest to Adelaide was characteristic of that same thoughtfulness for her appearance as in the days of the " geraniums "—it was a very beautiful lace veil.

In the winter of 1881 Adelaide was again attacked by illness. It was plain to see that " the sword was wearing out the sheath." Yet, after several weeks of suffering, she rallied and returned to her work. I was with her the day on which she left Boston to join the company at Chicago. The power of will carried her far beyond her strength, and a sad foreboding was in

the air as we parted. The foreboding was
soon confirmed. She made a brave strug-
gle to fulfil her engagements, but it was
not to be, and the winter of 1882 she spent
at the Tremont House in Boston, where
she received every attention. Miss Cowing was her constant companion, and her
family and friends were near. Adelaide
frequently drove to see me, as, in consequence of a fall on the ice, I was unable
to leave the house. She could stay, perhaps, only a few minutes, but would say as
she did of the musical studies, "I must
take you in at my eyes." Later in the
season we were more together, and I took
tea one evening with her at her rooms.
She, indeed, was "given to hospitality."
Although she put a cheerful courage on,
yet the trial she had to bear was a hard
one. The arrangement with Miss Ober
was satisfactory, and every week she
was losing pecuniary reward. She had
undertaken to build a large addition to

the house, and make expensive improvements at Marshfield, which added to her anxieties. The results of these changes, which included great conveniences for the family, and more ample accommodations for her friends, were anticipated by her with an interest that never flagged.

Before she left town for New York, and from thence to return to Marshfield, Adelaide and Matilde spent one evening with us. Although much changed outwardly by illness, Adelaide retained all her own depth of affection and magnetic fascination. Her descriptions of people and places were as vivid as ever, and her conversation never more brilliant. The evening had none of the sadness of a coming separation: it was full of life and light. She spoke of the pleasure she anticipated of visiting us at our summer home among the mountains, and once more her beautiful voice thrilled through our library, which had so often been filled by its

melody.   It lifted us beyond the clouds
that had seemed to obscure the present,
and gave us a glimpse of that future of
love and peace into which she was so
soon to enter.

On her return to Marshfield she found
the additions to the house, and all the
improvements she had planned, carried
out.   She spoke of many happy years to
come, and visits from her friends — dreams
which were pleasant, though not to be
realized.   Notwithstanding her extreme
weakness and suffering, her indomitable
spirit was not overcome; yet the fact that
she might not recover was really seldom
absent from her mind.   Such fluctuations
are not unfrequent.   The human heart
would sink indeed if it had not some
moments in which earthly hope mingled
with heavenly trust.   One little anecdote
of these last days at Marshfield gives us
herself " fading in music."   Arvilla being
occupied in another room, Adelaide was

left alone for some time. When her sister hurried back and expressed her regret at being so long absent, the reply was, "Oh, do not be troubled; I have had such a nice sing all to myself, not loud enough to be heard, but a nice sing. I went over 'Oh, rest in the Lord,' and something else, and I had such a quiet, pleasant time."

A letter written in August is full of hope and of trust. As we read the words there is such tenderness and pathos running through them that we are reminded of "Bunyan's delightful dream," and of the "sure token" the messenger gave Christiana — "an arrow with a point sharpened by love, let easily into her heart, which by degrees wrought so effectually with her that at the appointed time she must be gone."

MARSHFIELD, July 14, 1882.

DEAR MRS. WATERSTON, — I trust the air of Whitefield has done Mr. Waterston good, and that he has steadily improved.

I am getting on slowly but surely; but, oh dear, I have been very ill. I do not think they have told you how ill. They had to send for Dr. Wesselhoeft. He came on Friday, and returned and came again, staying over Sunday. I thought the end had come. I wished to live; but I was able to say, "Thy will, not mine, be done."

I have much to be thankful for, and I am thankful. I think, what shall I render unto the Lord for all his benefits to me?

I wish you could have seen the devotion of every one here, — such care, such nursing, and everything so pleasant around me. I am in my new room, and it has a charming view. Dear Alfred laid out flower-beds so that I could enjoy them at a distance. My bed was rolled each day close to the window so that I could see everything. Then the apple-trees were in bloom, one large tree looking right into my room. I cannot tell you how I enjoyed everything, though burning up with fever, and then so weak afterwards that I could do nothing for myself. I would exclaim continually, How lovely everything is! how grateful I am! I had felt sorry sometimes this winter that I had gone to the expense of making changes in the house, as I was under such heavy expenses, and had lost the whole winter. But I am glad now when I see how comfortable everything is ; we have a real home. Some four weeks ago I felt rather discouraged that I did not get along as quickly as I hoped. Dr. Wesselhoeft wrote to Matilde very encouragingly, but said "everything disagreeable must be kept from her ; she must make every effort to cast off care ; in fact, she must be very, very good." Well, I try to follow his directions, but it is hard not to feel anxious. The losses three years ago and this winter have been very serious, just as I thought everything was getting easy for me, so that sometimes I am a little low-spirited, but it does not last long, for I think how ungrateful I am, and then I pray, and great peace and comfort comes to me.

I have been obliged to come to a decision, and that is, it would be folly to think of singing next winter. I have sent word to Miss Ober, and I hope she may engage Matilde in my place, but I cannot help feeling anxious. When I am troubled it makes me ill, for I am not able to bear even any little troubles. You see what I mean, that I must get away at whatever cost. I must have some one with me. Arvilla has offered to go, but it is hard to separate her from Adrian. I am sure leading a quiet life I shall be ready for work next year. I shall try to sail in a

French steamer, on the 9th of August, from New York, go to Paris, where I shall rest a few days, then to Gastien in Austria. I hope to pass the winter in Nice or Mentone. That is what I wish to do. I know I could not stand the winter here doing nothing.

And now I have wearied you enough, but I wanted to tell you all.

With much love, your

ADELAIDE PHILLIPPS.

Under date of August 4th, 1882, I received her last letter: —

MARSHFIELD, August 4, 1882.

DEAR MRS. WATERSTON, — I hope to sail on Wednesday, on the Amerique, French line. My passage is secured. Arvilla goes with me. I want to remain away a year, but it will depend upon what my expenses are ; at all events I can stay six months. I feel it is the only thing to do. I cannot bear anything, and am very easily put back. So although I am not strong the doctor agrees with me it is best to leave at once. Then I shall have a pleasanter passage than later. I propose leaving here on Tuesday, taking the night train to New York, resting a few hours, and sail at two o'clock P. M. I will let you hear from me on my arrival. I am going to

Carlsbad first, as the waters are the thing for me to take. I trust Mr. Waterston is better. With love to both, I am,

Yours ever,

ADELAIDE PHILLIPPS.

The voyage seemed to recruit her strength. She always enjoyed the sea, and had made several voyages across the Atlantic merely for rest and recuperation after a fatiguing season.

Dr. Eckart of Marshfield crossed the ocean and remained with them until they left Paris.

After a few days rest Adelaide and Mrs. Adrian Phillipps reached Carlsbad, and took apartments at Königs Villa, a *pension* for invalids. The situation of the house pleased Adelaide, who was interested in the views from her room. One day, standing at the window looking at the mountain opposite, up whose side wound a pathway, she said to Arvilla, " I always think of Linda di Chamouni here, and seem to see Pierotto climbing up that path with his hurdy-gurdy on his back after leaving Linda." Adelaide took the waters, and was very much cheered by the hope of recovery, but the anxious sister watching her saw there was very little real improvement, yet no change so serious as to authorize a telegram to be sent to America. A few weeks thus passed, until suddenly, on October 3, 1882, the change came, and Adelaide Phillipps was gone. The stab of the telegram struck many hearts, and some were pierced as with a sword. To many it was the loss of a great singer, to others the parting from a dear friend, with whom much of their life went quite away. The press teemed with notices of her gifts, and paid every tribute to her noble character.

Meanwhile, alone in a far land, Mrs. Adrian Phillipps, who, as the young Arvilla, cheered Adelaide in Italy and was with her in her first professional triumphs, now closed her eyes upon this world. Like a guardian angel she smoothed the bed of death until the greater angel received the spirit. Those who know what it is to meet bereavement in a foreign land can sympathize in the trial Mrs. Phillipps had to encounter. She was placed in a very painful position, having to make all the sad final arrangements for removing the remains to America.

Friends, however, are always raised up in our dire need, God never leaving us without a witness of His care. Two gentlemen at that time residing at Carlsbad, Mr. Riley and Mr. Robert Johnson, recognized the difficulties Mrs. Phillipps had to encounter, came forward and assisted her through painful duties, and took the place of brothers. Such an opportunity of extending kindness does not often occur in life. Where it is so faithfully fulfilled the act carries its own reward, but the gratitude awakened is

cordially acknowledged.   Mr. Johnson
attended Mrs. Phillipps on the sad
journey to Bremen, from whence, after
some delay of the ship, she finally sailed
for America.   And now Adelaide was
again on the ocean:—

> " Calm on the seas, and silver sleep
>   The waves that sway themselves to rest,
>   And dead calm in that noble breast,
> Which heaves but with the heaving deep."

At last the ship came to port and the
voyage was over.

The funeral services were held in King's
Chapel, where the Rev. Mr. Foote pre-
ceded the bier covered with flowers,
uttering the uplifting words of the burial
service.   Solemn and appropriate music
was heard, heartfelt prayers offered,
the immortal words of the fifteenth chap-
ter of 1 Corinthians read, and then Mr.
Foote, returning to the desk, made a most
tender and impressive address.   Music
again filled the chapel, and with the bene-
diction the crowd dispersed.

After the services were over, the casket, which contained all that had been mortal of Adelaide Phillipps, was carried to Marshfield, and once more she rested in the home she so much loved, surrounded by her brothers and sisters. Once more they met together.

The next day the weary form was laid in the quiet "God's acre," at Marshfield, but the soul that animated it had risen upward and onward, where a new song was put into her lips.

APPENDIX.

APPENDIX.

IT was the wish of the Phillipps family that the services at their sister's funeral should be conducted by the Rev. Mr. Waterston; as it was impossible for him to comply with their kind request, his friend, the Rev. H. W. Foote, pastor of King's Chapel, fulfilled the duty in the most tender and sympathetic manner. The following letter expresses the feeling awakened in his mind on the occasion : —

BOSTON, February 18, 1883.

MY DEAR MRS. WATERSTON, — I am led by your preparation of the Memoir of Miss Phillipps to wish afresh that it had been in your power to be present at the funeral services, which were held in King's Chapel, so that you might have felt the atmosphere of sympathy and sorrow which pervaded the great throng to a very unusual degree. I have rarely seen an assembly so moved by a common feeling, or so evidently touched with a sense of personal loss. Every variety of social condition was represented there, and friends ranging from the closest kindred to those who only knew Miss Phillipps as one who has stirred their souls by her beautiful and noble gift.

157

All seemed to be there simply because they could not stay away from the last opportunity to show that they loved her. It was such a tribute of affection as it is given to few either to deserve or to win.

Faithfully yours,
HENRY W. FOOTE.

FUNERAL SERVICE.

At midday on October 25, 1882, the last rites were observed at King's Chápel, which was thronged. Beautiful flowers, gifts from personal and professional friends, profusely bestowed, were arranged with great taste in the chancel. The pure white and green so largely predominated that the decoration seemed modest and retiring. Preceding the bier strewed with blossoms, the Rev. Mr. Foote commenced the solemn service. On entering the desk he read the thirty-ninth and ninetieth psalms, with the alternate verses given as responses by the choir. After reading the regular church service, Mr. Foote spoke as follows : —

" In this solemn presence we listen for a voice that on earth is forever still, and out of the silence do we not seem, my friends, to hear that voice bidding us ' rest in the Lord, and wait patiently for him.' It is well that here in this city, so associated with her early and later life, — on this spot so close to that where her pure genius first rose shining as a star, — this great company of friends who knew and loved her should gather for this tender memorial rite; and with them are many others of that wider company who knew and loved her in as true, though not in as close a way, to whom she had spoken through her divine gift, to comfort, to uplift, to console, — many of whom probably associate some of the purest, most uplifted moments of their lives with the tones that revealed to them the divine meaning that may be hidden in human hearts. It is well, I say, that we should pause, and look to God, and be grateful for what this life hath given. We do not here recount the triumphs of an art, whose triumphs at such an hour as this must turn to bitter ashes unless there is character behind them; but we may well rejoice that art was interpreted to us by one who was pure, faithful, true, noble, and womanly. Her love for her art was of the highest sort, so that she became an interpreter, for those who listened, of the divine secret in the centre of every human life, the purpose God has for every human soul.

"Here was one who took God's gift as His own, reverently, and used it in that spirit, appreciating the great privilege of having this gift, through which to speak to other human hearts and help them on their way. Here is one who, though gone from us, leaves the world the eternal lesson of an upright and consecrated life. This is the simple truth, and because it is so, I repeat the written words of one who knew her well, and who ought rather as her friend of many years to express in my stead, in the presence to-day, the emotion of this great company. ' The thought of her noble character rises before me. I think of her devotion, her self-sacrifice, always faithful and true. Her voice was a worthy expression of all that was good, giving utterance to the sacred words of truth and holy cheer. Do we not hear it even now as she receives a crown from the Lord's hands in the midst of heaven.'

"As here we lay upon the bier the wreath of respect — of honor for one who has kept unstained the pure type of American womanhood, — the wreath of love and personal tenderness springing strongly and deeply from many hearts, we hearken for the keynote of her life ; and let her own words, written a few months ago in the confidence of friendship, speaking in the sacred privacy of this hushed and sorrowing assembly, reveal to us what that keynote was. ' I thought,' she says, ' the end was near. I wished to live, but was able to say "Thy will, not mine, be done." I am sometimes low-spirited, but it does not last long ; I think how ungrateful I am, and then I pray, and great peace and comfort come to me.' Great peace and comfort ! Oh, sorrowing friends, think not that in vain we wait here for that comfort and peace. This life ended, as it would seem, prematurely, and, as a broken harmony here below, is continued in the higher mansion, where the Great Composer can call forth at His will what note he pleases from the soul of His child. Though the divine harmony may die on earth it is only that the heavenly song may go on forever and forever."

At the conclusion of his remarks prayer was again offered by Mr. Foote, and then Mrs. E. C. Fenderson sang Mendelssohn's "Oh, rest in the Lord."

Afterwards the quartette, "Their sun shall no more go down" was sung by Mrs. West, Mrs. Butler, Mrs. Barry, and Mrs. Sawyer.

LAST TRIBUTE TO THE GREAT ARTIST BY HER MARSHFIELD FRIENDS AND NEIGHBORS.

[From the Marshfield Mail.]

MARSHFIELD, October 28, 1882.

The remains of Adelaide Phillips arrived here last Wednesday afternoon, after the services at King's Chapel, Boston. The casket was tenderly conveyed to her late residence, amid the tears of regret of her Marshfield admirers and friends, to await the morrow, when they pay the last tribute of love and respect to the great artist and kind friend of the Marshfield people.

Not since thirty years ago this same month have the sympathies of the residents of the old historic town of Marshfield been so awakened by the death of one of its citizens. An hour previous to the appointed time of service the friends assembled, filling all available space in the house, to mingle their tears with the tears of her immediate relatives.

After impressive services, conducted by the Rev. E. Allen, of Marshfield, the remains were carried to the old Winslow burying-ground, and interred in a beautiful lot near the Webster monument.   Thus has Marshfield paid its last tribute of respect, friendship, and love to one who will be missed from the circle of public and private life.   And deep are the sympathies felt for the members of a household, who mourn the loss of a kind friend and a much-beloved sister.

[*From the Old Colony Memorial.*]

IN MEMORIAM.

OH, pleasant homestead in the dell,
  My heart goes out to thee,
And seeks to lay upon thy hearth
  A stranger's sympathy.

I mourn the links now rent in twain,
  By death's relentless hand ;
Which makes a circle widely known,
  A broken-hearted band.

Bend, larches, bend your lordly head
  And drop your leaflets sere,
In sad and noiseless showers upon
  The solemn, lowly bier.

Of one to whom the whole wide world
   Its choicest tribute pays
With tears and sighs and heartfelt grief,
   And well-remembered lays.

Ye maples, sheltering the panes
   Of that now hallowed room,
Where our sweet singer lies at rest,
   Amidst earth's fragrant bloom.

Reach out your arms and keep within,
   Stray echoes of some song,
Which will repeat themselves to us,
   When life's strange days seem long.

Lift her, ye bearers, tenderly,
   And move with reverend tread
Through the worn gates that shut within
   The city of the dead.

'Tis but an humble burial,
   Yet angels bend to see
The tear-wet eyes, the pale, bared brows,
   And sob of sympathy.

Room, Mother Earth, make room for her,
   Whose short fair reign is o'er,
We who go with her to the end,
   Must leave her at thy door.

The golden gates are just ajar,
  The veil between how thin;
But we can only stand without,
  And watch her pass within.

God's ways are just; our voices raise,
  A Jubilate sweet.
For one who sits as Mary sat,
  Close at the Master's feet.

At rest in heaven! Oh precious boon,
  To each and all the same;
God gave, God took, God will restore,
  Thrice blessed be His name.

                    MARIE OLIVER.

OCTOBER 26, 1882.

TRIBUTE FROM THE IDEAL OPERA COMPANY.

The death of Miss Phillipps is the first that has occurred among the principals of the Boston Ideal Opera Company since it was formed. The following letter has been forwarded to her family: —

               "BOSTON, MASS., Oct. 5, 1882.

To the members of the family of the late
    Adelaide Phillipps :

" In the sudden and grievous loss which you have sustained in the death of your sister Adelaide, we, as members of the company of which she was one, desire to express our sincere sympathy with you, and the keen sense of our own sorrow, at this, the first irrevocable break of our original members. By what she was, in her dignified, generous, genial, and inspiring presence, her ever-ready aid, her never-waning enthusiasm for her profession, her exalted standard of art, her vital dramatic power, and her glorious voice — by all these fine qualities, blended with a pure, sympathetic and womanly spirit, which shone so brightly in friendly intercourse and daily association, we can estimate what she was to you in the closer and dearer family relations, and appreciate what an incalculable loss is that which you have sustained.

With repeated expressions of heartfelt sympathy in your affliction, we are,

Yours sincerely,

E. H. Ober.	Marie Stone.
W. H. MacDonald.	M. W. Whitney.
Tom Karl.	George Frothingham.
Mary Beebe.	Geraldine Ulmar.
H. C. Barnabee.	W. H. Fessenden.
Jesse Burton.	S. L. Studley."

The following extracts are made from the tributes to Miss Phillipps which appeared in the newspapers of the day. They contained accounts of her professional career, many of which are given in the foregoing pages, and are therefore omitted here : —

[*From the Brooklyn Eagle.*]

. . . " She died early, for she was under fifty years of age, the time of life called by Victor Hugo ' the youth of old age,' and in the fulness of a noble fame. For a quarter of a century she has delighted audiences in the concert-room and opera. She was a woman whose public success was a gratification to her, but her life-work was not confined to her public career, and the motive behind her was not self-advancement. . . . This spirit which characterized her influenced every audience that she appeared before, and the welcome accorded Miss Phillipps was something more than applause — it was honest friendship for the woman."

[*From the Boston Home Journal.*]

"The death of Miss Phillipps has caused widespread grief. For many a year a whole people have learned to look upon her as exclusively their own. Her fame was created by a life-work as varied as it was brilliant, and it was conspicuous as the life of a pure and noble woman.

She was a great vocalist, and she could not have been this without ample and well directed culture of mind. Listening to her rendering of oratoric music, we were always impressed by the spirit which lived in every sentence she uttered, for she was above virtuosity, and her conception of art became clear and elevated to the highest degree."

[*From the Boston Daily Advertiser.*]

... " The lyric stage loses one of its most brilliant luminaries by the death of Miss Phillipps. As a contralto singer she ranked among the first. As an oratorio singer she had few rivals in England or this country. Although she has been before the public for well nigh a quarter of a century, her voice retained to a remarkable degree its original strength and purity, and her artistic powers up to the last showed no trace of abatement."

[*From the Boston Evening Transcript.*]

... " Adelaide Phillipps' career was not unlike that of many other dramatic artists. But there was so much in it that was a source of pride to those who knew her, and, more than all, it included many incidents that were at once examples and encouragement to others in the profession. . . . The news of her death will be received by thousands of people who knew her only on the stage with a feeling akin to that one experiences in learning the death of a personal friend. . . . She fought the battle of life nobly, and all her triumphs were won without a stain on her womanly reputation. Though not born in America, we still can claim her as one who represented in her career the best elements of independence and self-reliance, which are the genuine characteristics of the women of America."

[*From the Boston Commonwealth.*]

. . . " In the sweet and wholesome career of this distinguished woman there is much to encourage ,all young singers who are ambitious to attain the summit of artistic heights.   Her private life was as pure and blameless as her works were grand and ennobling. Her steady industry, high aspirations, devotion to duty, and her unselfish efforts in behalf of struggling brother and sister professionals — all attributes of a noble nature — will be long remembered by all who came within the sweet magnetism of her presence. Although her song is forever stilled, its echoes will long remain in the hearts of humanity."

EXTRACTS FROM PRIVATE LETTERS.

Many letters have been received while this record was in preparation.   Indeed the expressions quoted from a few only embody the feeling manifested by many.

Among the letters from her friends in New York, are those from Mrs. Dr. Doremus, Mrs. Clarence Seward, and Mrs. Minna Godwin Goddard, in whose homes Adelaide was often a welcome guest.   A few words from Mrs. Goddard combine the thoughts of those who loved her : " Adelaide came to us last May, very weak from recent illness, but always charming, and so constantly interested in others, and fearful of giving trouble, that it was a pleasure to care for her, and delightful to have her in the house. We were more than ever impressed during this visit with the generosity and truth of her character. Her death is a great bereavement to us, and we cannot yet realize how it can be that we shall see her no more.".

From Mrs. Ford : " It grieves one to think of that noble voice silent, and that loving heart no longer beating its steady rhythms of devotion and constancy. Yet her memory is very sweet to me, and I am comforted to believe that she was loved while on earth and mourned now that she has passed on. She was taken away before infirmity changed her or time had enfeebled her powers. Indeed, her life and death seem fortunate to me, for though she had much to contend with, and many disappointments, she conquered circumstances and won many triumphs."

From Miss Monell : " As I think of Adelaide and her exquisite sense of duty, her justice and sweet patience, her tender womanliness, and unwavering loyalty, I wonder if there ever was a lovelier soul on earth, or one more fitted for heaven."

The record of the public and private life of Adelaide Phillipps cannot be closed more impressively than by repeating these words of T. W. Parsons : —

REALITY.

" Lift me, Lord Jesus, for the time is nigh,
When I must climb unto thy cross at last.
The world fades out, its lengthening shadows fly ;
Earth's pomp is passing, and the music's past !
Phantoms flock round me, multiplying fast;
Nothing seems tangible; the good I thought
Most permanent hath perished.   Come away,
Oh sated spirit, from the vacant scene,
The curtain drops upon the spun-out play ;
The benches are deserted.   Let us go.
Forget the foolish clown, the King, the Queen,
The idle story with its love and woe :
I seem to stand before a minster screen,
And hear faint organs in the distance blow."